RONNIE

A MONEY, POWER & SEX STORY

MONEY,POWER & SEX
BOOK SEVEN

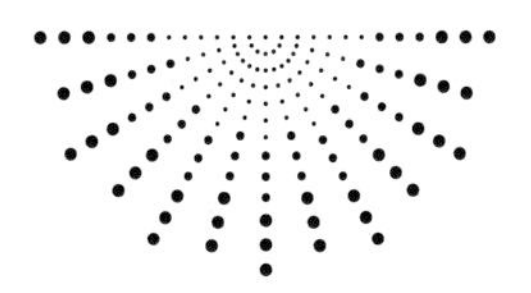

NORIAN LOVE

4/25 - 4/27/23

This is a work of fiction. Names, characters businesses, organizations, places, events and incidents are either the product of the author's imagination or used facetiously. Any resemblance to actual persons, living or dead, events or locales is entirely coincidental.

ISBN: 978-1-7366707-9-8

ISBN: 1-7366707-9-4

For Ta Ta
Love Always

ACKNOWLEDGMENTS

I am humbled and honored to have the opportunity to acknowledge the immense support and contributions that have gone into the creation of my latest novel, "Ronnie: A Money, Power & Sex Story". As an author, I have always believed that the success of any book is largely dependent on the support and encouragement of those around me. I would like to take this opportunity to express my heartfelt gratitude to everyone who has played a role in bringing this book to life.

First and foremost, I would like to express my deepest appreciation to my readership. Without your unwavering support, my stories would not have been heard, and my voice would not have been amplified. Your feedback, encouragement, and engagement have been a source of inspiration and motivation throughout this journey. You have made me a better writer, and for that, I am forever grateful.

I would also like to extend my heartfelt thanks to my support staff, including my editors, agents, publishers, and publicists. Your dedication, expertise, and commitment to excellence have been invaluable to the success of this book. Your tireless efforts behind the scenes have allowed me to focus on my craft and to create a work that I am proud of. You have been my partners in this journey, and I could not have done it without you.

Finally, I would like to thank my family and friends for their love, support, and understanding. Writing can be a solitary and demanding pursuit, and it is only through the unwavering support of those closest to me that I have been able to persevere. You have been my pillars of strength, my sounding boards, and my cheerleaders, and for that, I am eternally grateful.

In closing, I would like to say that "Ronnie: A Money, Power & Sex Story" is not just my book, but our book. It is a product of the collective effort and energy of a community of people who believe in the power of storytelling. Thank you for being a part of that community and for joining me on this journey. I hope you enjoy reading this book as much as I enjoyed writing it.

From Norian,
With Love.

STARTING OVER

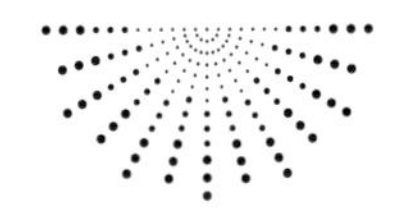

ew York

"Good morning, New York City. We are The Breakfast Club. I'm your host, DJ En—"

Click.

Nichelle turned off the alarm. She was already in the bathroom getting dressed for her appointment with the gynecologist later in the day.

She was putting on black spandex tights as she caught sight of herself in the mirror. She took a moment to look at her stomach – a barely discernible bump had developed. It was the first time she'd noticed it.

She gently rubbed her stomach, somber as she put on an oversized, ruffled plum-colored sweater she'd picked up from Old Navy. A black cashmere scarf was her ultimate accessory as she finished getting ready.

She walked into the lounge room to see her brother, Nicolas, watching TV.

"Hey sis, the news is on. They're talking about H-town again!" he yelled. She rolled her eyes as his voice echoed through the apartment.

She'd come all this way to get away from her life in Houston, and now it was national news.

"Chelle!" he repeated.

She sighed and shook her head. "I'm coming, Nick," she muttered.

She finished putting on her gold mini-hoop earrings while glancing at the 65-inch flat screen television hanging on the wall.

Ever since she'd left the city of Houston, she'd found herself unable to avoid anything that had to do with the news there. The reality was, with everything going on, Houston was the hot topic for news channels all over the country at the moment.

There were still a lot of loose ends for her to tie up, and they weren't going anywhere, so for the time being she was reluctantly in-the-know from a distance.

"They're not messing around in H-town, are they?" her brother bellowed as he leaned into the black leather couch he was sitting on.

"Apparently not," she responded.

The news focused on the uproar about the latest protest, and ended with the most recent bank robbery. This time an entire ATM was stolen. It was Donovan's handiwork, no doubt about it.

"Authorities say the ATM was holding at least one hundred and seventy thousand dollars in cash at the time. No witnesses have come forward at this time." The anchor continued to describe what sounded like a clean getaway.

Nichelle did the math in her head.

A hundred and seventy racks? Even with a partner, that's almost 90 grand a piece. Damn, he's putting in work. He's probably working with Trouble. They need to be careful, or he's gonna end up in jail again.

"Chelle?"

"Huh?"

She snapped back to reality when her brother continued to talk. "I said that robbery could never happen in New York. The streets are too tight, and the cops are everywhere."

"Oh…yeah, I guess you're right." Her mind – and secretly her heart – was still stuck on thoughts of Donovan.

Her brother continued. "People are saying the bank robberies are 'coz of that police shooting. The mayor is considering implementing a city-wide curfew, and instead of looting, people have escalated to bank robberies. That's some crazy shit, ain't it?"

"Yeah…crazy," she replied half-heartedly.

"If you ask me, I think the banks are just trying to cash in on some insurance money and are blaming black folk while they get paid."

"Nick, they're going to get the insurance money either way, and they wouldn't have to blame anyone. You just think that because there are no witnesses."

"See, that's why it's an inside job. Nobody's that good to steal an entire ATM and make a clean getaway? Come on, sis!" He seemed excited that the robber had gotten away with the crime.

His perspective annoyed her. "I don't think it was an inside job. You're giving the people who work at the banks too much credit."

"Well, all I know is, whoever it was just made bank. If they ever find the robbers, and it turns out it's a brother, they gonna put his face all over the TV and interview his momma, her momma, and dig up his great grandmomma to interview her too."

"Nick, there's already more than enough happening in Houston to try to make this into a race issue."

"First of all, everything is a race issue."

"Oh, here you go."

"No, I'm serious, Chelle. You gotta question the timing. Why is it that banks started being robbed quicker after this shooting? Come on, sis, you gotta admit it's odd timing."

As crazy as he was talking, his last statement was right. She had a strong feeling the bank robberies were directly related to the shooting – and though her brother didn't know it, she was connected to it all. She was certain Donovan Brown was the culprit behind the recent rash of bank robberies. She cringed at the notion that he was taking advantage of the chaos behind the social injustice rhetoric to hide his motives

Gotta admit, this cocky motherfucker is a genius.

There was no way the police had made a connection to a person or crew yet, considering how overwhelmed they were with the protests.

It was dangerous, it was self-serving.

It was brilliant.

It was Donovan.

If only he could use that brain of his for good, maybe none of this shit would be happening.

She was fighting an inescapable reality. The robberies, the shooting, and Lucas being in the hospital were her fault. She knew in her soul that Donovan was hard at work trying to recoup the stolen money she'd spent. His actions were not only going to land him back in jail, but they were undermining a serious issue in the nation, and she was feeling the weight of it all.

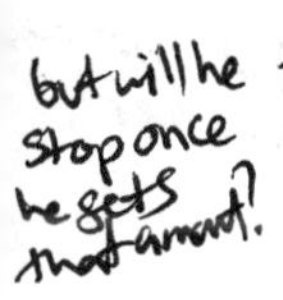

It wasn't the only thought to haunt her though. She was also worried about the man on the other end of the bullet that had sparked all of this.

She prayed silently. *Lord, please let Lucas live.*

She knew that, had she never called Lucas over to her house that night, he wouldn't have been shot, and the city wouldn't have erupted. Not to mention, had she not spent the money, none of this would be happening.

She wanted to reach out to Donovan, to convince him to stop what he was doing. The consequences of his actions didn't matter to him. He didn't see or care that his actions would lead to cops becoming more aggressive and, eventually, someone else would get shot or killed.

He only cared about one thing: his money.

This is all my fault.

The guilt was inescapable – a growing pit in her conscience that was causing her nausea.

"I'm Helen of motherfucking Troy," she muttered to herself.

"You say something, sis?"

"What?"

"You just said something about Helen or someone…who's that?"

"A real unfortunate bitch."

"Wait, what? Who are you talking about?"

"Forget it, Nick. I was just thinking about some work stuff. In fact, I'm about to leave to get my day started."

She wanted the conversation to be over, but her brother pressed on. "I didn't know you guys had an office here. Where is it?"

"Oh. Um...yeah, I'm working remote. I'm just leaving to run a few errands. Hey, do you need anything while I'm out?" she asked, hoping her brother would move on.

"Some pork rinds would be on point. There's a bodega about a block from here. The spicy kind."

"Okay, one bag of high blood pressure. Got it," she mocked as she leaned in and kissed him on the forehead.

As she was opening the door, Nick called out again. "Hey, Chelle?"

"Ycah?"

"You sure you're okay?"

"I'm fine. I just...I hate everything that's happening in Houston, that's all." She sounded unconvincing, which her brother clearly picked up on.

"Well, I mean, if you want to talk...I know we usually don't do that kind of stuff, but that's...well, I'm—"

"I'm fine, Nick," she interjected, saving her brother from his half-hearted offer.

"Okay. Hey, bring me back a tropical soda, too. Doesn't matter what kind."

"So, one bag of high blood pressure and a bottle of diabetes juice. Got it."

"Hey, Chelle. Didn't you live somewhere in that area in Houston?"

"Umm... it all kinda looks the same now. Houston is a big city."

A quick Google search could have exposed her paper thin lie, if he truly cared. But then again, they'd never been terribly close. There was no point in telling him since he would pretend to be interested, only to eventually make it about him and why leaving Houston was the best thing he'd ever done.

"Yeah, well, it's a good thing you left when you did. Who knows what could've happened? This kind of stuff is the reason I left."

Right on cue.

She bit the inside of her cheek. It didn't matter what the issue was; Nicolas Myers was going to say New York was better than Houston, and that's why he left.

Nichelle looked at him blankly. "Yeah, you're right. Well, at any rate, I'm out."

She picked up her keys and left the brownstone.

As she walked down the front steps, the cold brisk air quickly snapped her mind back to her own issues. The gravity of her circumstances became heavier: she was in love with two men who couldn't be any more different from each other.

One was a victim, in the wrong place at the wrong time, and the other prided himself on being the living embodiment of 'wrong place, wrong time'.

She put her headphones on and listened to her *Boss up Bitch* playlist. Window Seat by Ericka Badu was up first. *Perfect.*

She casually strolled down the New York pavement, a fresh change of pace from Houston. There was always something to do in this city. It was hard not to love it.

She smiled and turned up the volume.

Her life felt like a glass of lemonade with more lemon than sugar. When Lucas had told her he was happy with Ronnie, of all people, she'd wanted to shoot him herself. And when she'd found the engagement ring, for a split second part of her wanted to see him suffer, a thought she'd instantly regretted. She wondered if she'd willed it all into existence.

Me and D had a good thing, but so did me and Luke. Damn it.

She wished she could talk to them, or even just one of them.

She knew she'd made several mistakes – some unforgivable – but so had they.

She replayed that last night over in her head every waking hour, and she needed to let out her frustration.

I gotta talk to someone.

She wanted a male's perspective, without judgment.

It couldn't be her brother.

She thought about the unsympathetic paramedic when she'd taken Luke to the hospital. *He had it all wrong. Lucas would never hit me.*

She needed to tell him.

She looked through her purse and found his card.

Gregory Tribett – Paramedic.

She called the number.

This is stupid.

She considered hanging up when the call finally connected. "This is Greg."

"Greg? Hi, is this… I'm sorry, I got the wrong nu—"

"Nichelle? Is that you?"

"Hey, it's me. Hi." she said, surprised that he knew it was her.

"How are you doing?" he continued, softening the uneasiness she was feeling.

"I'm…fine, I guess. How are you?"

"I'm doing well. Just finished my shift. It was crazy today. Are you sure you're okay?"

"I'm just…"

"Just what?" he persisted.

"I'm just…surprised you remember me, that's all."

"Well, it's not every day you transport someone who becomes national news. Besides, I gave you my card, hoping you'd call."

"I guess it was a pretty memorable night."

Nichelle chuckled somewhat nervously. She wasn't sure why she was on the phone with Greg.

"Well, all things considered, how have you been?" he chimed in, breaking the silence that was growing.

"I'm fine. I've just…been doing me, ya know?"

"I feel you on that. I look for you from time to time at the hospital, since I drop off there so frequently. I figure you must be up there a lot checking on Lucas."

"Actually, I haven't been to the hospital since that night."

"Oh…well I'm glad you called. I was hoping I'd get a chance to apologize for what I said to you that night. I wasn't trying to judge. I was concerned. You're a beautiful woman and I've seen a lot of abuse on this job—"

"It wasn't like that, and it certainly wasn't Lucas."

"Was it one of the co—"

"I'm not in the right frame of mind to talk about that night, if you don't mind."

"Right, no doubt. I can respect that. Maybe you'd like to talk in person, perhaps over coffee? Not trying to hit on you – sorry, that's a poor choice of words. I'm not trying… Look, I just want to make sure you're okay."

"Why do you care? You don't know me at all."

"That's true, and I'm not trying to upset you. I just—"

"You were just judging me. You think I got out of an abusive relationship and ran to another city to avoid dealing with my life? Well, I didn't."

"No, Nichelle, that's not what I was thinking at all. I'm concerned about you, but—"

"You know what? This was a mistake. I have to go."

"Nichelle, I swear I—"

"Goodbye, Greg."

Click.

She hung up the phone, not allowing him to insult her any further.

"The nerve of these dudes," she muttered to herself.

By the time she reached the front door of the doctor's office, she'd received a text.

Nichelle, it's Greg. I want to apologize. I wasn't trying to make you upset. You're right, I don't know you. I want to get to know you, if you'll allow it. The night you were at the hospital, I told you I have a daughter and I'm a paramedic. It's in my nature to help people. But I also think you could use a friend right now. I apologize if I crossed a line. It wasn't my intent.

Nichelle deleted the message and decided to just ignore Greg from now on.

She took the elevator up to the third floor and walked into suite 301.

There were several couples in the waiting room. A black man in his mid-thirties was whispering sweet nothings to his wife's stomach, pressing a plush basketball toy against her bump.

She couldn't help but think of Lucas. That's the kind of father he would be, if her child was his. He'd always wanted to be a father.

The same was true of Donovan.

What the hell have I done?

As her thoughts weighed on her, the nurse called her. "Nichelle Myers?"

She stood up to walk to the second waiting room as the nurse motioned her towards the large oak door. They ushered her into waiting room 4. She scoffed when she realized that this room was much bigger than the first.

This is pointless. What's the point of leaving one waiting room just to sit in another?

There were several charts on the walls about women's reproductive system: making sure you test for sexually transmitted diseases regularly, and mammograms.

After ten minutes, she became restless waiting and finally, out of sheer boredom, she responded to Greg's text.

Hey, no big, I'm just having a moment. We're good.

She hit send, and it wasn't long before she got a reply.

OK, so do over whenever you get back in town?

OK, sounds like a plan.

As she hit send, the doctor – a graying middle-aged white man with a distinct liver spot covering the outer edges of his orbital bone – finally walked in. He wore a lab coat and red-framed glasses.

About fucking time.

"Welcome back, Ms. Myers."

"Hi, Dr. Sinclair."

"How are you faring? I remember in our last appointment you had some spotting."

"I know you said it was normal, but I'm still spotting, and have been for a few days now. I just want to be sure."

The doctor smiled. "It's good that you're cautious. First-time parents always are – the good ones, at least. Lay down and I'll examine you."

The doctor checked her over and, after a quick internal examination, he said, "At the moment, there are no indications of anything wrong with the baby."

"What if…" She paused, embarrassed. The doctor waited for her to finish her sentence. "What if I had a few drinks…early in the pregnancy? Before I knew I was pregnant," she asked.

"How much are we talking, and how long ago? A glass of wine? A shot of whiskey?"

Nichelle couldn't admit that she had been on a drinking binge the night Lucas was shot. Instinctively, she lied. "Oh, this was much earlier, and I think it was a couple shots of tequila, maybe."

In truth, she'd had several Teriyaki Teas – made up of four kinds of hard liquor – the day before she came to New York. What's worse – since she'd been in New York, she'd had at least two more episodes similar.

In fact, she'd only stopped drinking once she'd noticed the spotting. She regretted it, and the subsequent nights. Another item to add to her list of sins, but not one she thought the child she was carrying should pay for. You want a baby with disabilities?! Cut it out!

"Well, Ms. Myers, I won't say alcohol is good for a baby. There are significant risk factors that are attributed with drinking at any point during the pregnancy."

"Yes, but this was before I knew I was pregnant."

"While that may be true, your awareness doesn't change the science. Your body is still carrying a baby, so not being aware of the pregnancy is irrelevant. If you've stopped drinking, the pregnancy risk is lowered, but it's still early. We'll keep monitoring you, and I can send the information back to your OB-GYN in Houston."

Nichelle was relieved at his response, though still slightly embarrassed. "Okay, well I'm not drinking anymore."

"I would hope not. To be perfectly clear, liquor will almost directly affect your fetus' health and wellbeing. No amount is safe."

"I get it doc. I wasn't aware, but I am now, thank you."

The doctor used his lab coat to clean his glasses. "Look, I've been doing this a long time. It's still early on, and your baby is still developing. There are several things you can do to promote healthy growth: good eating, prenatal vitamins. As long as you put your baby first, I think you're going to have a healthy child. Still, I do highly recommend we monitor the spotting as you continue on your journey."

"Thanks, doc," she said, her stress alleviated.

"I'm going to prescribe some prenatal vitamins, and ask you to come back in two weeks. When you leave, the receptionist will make the appointment and we can do another ultrasound then."

"Thank you, Dr. Sinclair."

When she walked out onto the street, the cool air greeted her. She tightened her scarf and walked down the road. She'd yet to eat all day and, taking the doctor's advice, she decided a good meal was in order. Around the corner from the hospital was a place called Russo's, a local bar and restaurant. It had a decent amount of traffic, which in New York meant the food was good.

She walked in and was greeted by a short Hispanic lady with dark hair. "Hello, welcome to Russo's. Would you like a table, or to sit at the bar?"

Nichelle looked around at the waiting customers. There were at least six people in front of her. "Yes, um, how long is the wait?"

"About twenty minutes."

"I'll sit at the bar."

She took her seat and began to look over the menu before she was interrupted by her phone vibrating. She pulled it out of her purse to see the news notification on the screen.

"Houston man shot by police to be placed in a medically-induced coma."

Nichelle froze.

Her mind immediately went to the night they shot Lucas.

Donovan hitting holes in her wall when he found out about the money she spent.

Lucas, her former lover, wanting nothing to do with her.

Now he was fighting for his life, because she couldn't resist her ex-lover who seemed to be intent on sending himself back to jail.

She thought about his family, the Kimbles, and how hurt they were the night they'd been notified, and even thought about Ronnie's pain and anguish, despite being a cold and heartless bitch.

The guilt that she was responsible for all of it weighed on her more every day.

As her emotions started to become too much to face, the bartender came over. "Welcome to Russo's. Would you like an appetizer, or anything to drink, or are you ready to order?"

Nichelle looked at the notification again and then at the bartender.

"Yes, Mark, I'd like a Long Island Iced Tea, please."

Back to drinking :(

1

THE COST OF SUCCESS

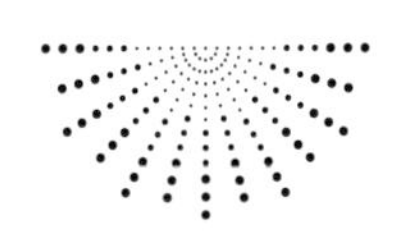

Click, click, click.

Ronnie pounded the sandstone tile with her black Christian Louboutin heels, each step punishing the floors of St. Luke's Hospital.

Her workday was over, but it was time to start her second shift. As she walked into the Neurological Intensive Care Unit ward for the fourth consecutive night. There looked to be no ending to this new routine.

She chuckled at the irony of spending her days crushing all her enemies as the undisputed star at Burrows Industries, yet her nights were spent in the most uncomfortable chair in St. Luke's Hospital, a place that unfortunately was becoming all-too-familiar.

She called for the elevator, promptly placing her hand under the antibacterial dispenser resting above the buttons. As the doors opened, a wave of relief came over her; there was no one in the elevator to make small talk with. It was a small victory, and she'd take them in any form at the moment.

She walked in and pressed the button for the third floor. She took a deep breath and looked at her engagement ring. It was flawless.

You got this girl.

She'd never liked hospitals. Things never seemed to turn out in her favor.

As she turned down the hallway of Lucas's ward, an alarm began to blare, nurses scrambling past her. "He's coding!" one yelled, as they quickly dashed past her.

Unfortunately, she knew all too well what the nurse meant. Coding meant someone was dying; a word she'd been praying she wouldn't hear again since the night the police had shot Lucas. She was relieved to see it wasn't Lucas since they were passing his room.

"I hate this place," she muttered.

Visiting a hospital never ended with good news. The sounds of misfortune, and the sounds of the hospital, were synonymous. She was too familiar with the various noises, and was even able to recognize what some of them meant.

She did not want to be here, witnessing people grasp life with the tiny amounts of energy they had remaining, but she had to be here. In fact, in the last few weeks, she'd realized there was no place for her to go besides this hospital. Lucas was here, and he was the only man she'd ever loved.

It had been three weeks since he'd been shot. He wasn't conscious, and it felt like a death. She'd grown accustomed to him making her laugh. His optimism was a ray of sunshine that had been dimmed, and wouldn't return until he did.

She was alone – something she used to enjoy, but now despised.

Despite her discomfort, she was here. The hospital made her physically nauseous; it also made her want to shower. It was clean enough, but knowing how much bacteria was likely around made her skin crawl. She obsessively used the antibacterial dispensers getting on and off the elevators, and in the hallways as she walked to visit her lover.

She walked into Lucas Kimble's room and located her usual chair. That and her makeshift bed were quickly becoming her most-hated objects, if only because she was getting used to them.

She glanced over at the machine recording his vitals. "I see your blood pressure is still slightly elevated, Mr. Kimble. You're gonna need to cut back on the salt," she mocked. "Heart rate is steady. You're making good progress, Mr. Kimble. But don't get up, just relax and rest."

In the past few weeks she'd learned to understand what the reading meant. Understanding them was one step close to Lucas waking up.

The sounds of the machines were disturbing her first few nights here, but now they'd become white noise to her sleep.

She glanced at the breathing machine to make sure that his oxygen levels were good; he was doing most of the breathing on his own, which was a good sign.

Immediately after the shooting, he'd relied heavily upon the machines, close to eighty percent. Tonight, the machine was only doing thirty-seven percent of the work, which means his lungs were getting stronger.

She glanced at him. Her fiancé for all intents and purposes, and the father of her child, but more than that, he was her counterbalance. A man she'd slowly allowed into her heart, a man who was changing her, even in his stillness. A man she wished would just wake the fuck up right now.

A movement beyond the doorway caught her attention at the nurse's workstation. A portly man with dark skin wearing blue scrubs and black square-framed glasses was sitting at a desk, working diligently.

He looked up and caught her eye, smiling. "Hi, Mrs. Kimble, he's been—"

"Jacob, I told you to call me Ronnie. Besides, I can't be Mrs. Kimble until this guy here wakes up." She rubbed the top of his head, his hair now growing unchecked.

"You're right. I'm sorry, Ronnie."

"No worries at all. Give me the latest on Lucas."

"Well, he's improving. He's healing from the gunshot wound, clotting well. There's a slight infection around the entry wound, but the antibiotics should take care of that. There's no way to say for certain, but there should be no neurological damage; his vitals are strong. His kidneys are working harder than we'd like, but he's been through a lot so that's to be expected. As far as the crack in his skull, the swelling hasn't gone down, but there's been no effect on brain activity. As you know, the doctors want to operate to see if they can reduce the swelling.

"But they don't have permission, right?"

"Correct. His parents are still denying the surgeons permission to operate."

"Great."

The doctors had increasingly pressured the family to operate on Lucas, to which his parents strongly objected. While his mother, Natalie, declined for spiritual reasons, his father, Walter, simply asked the right questions.

The doctors informed them that while they could guarantee nothing, there was an extremely high probability that he would heal naturally, albeit slowly. There was no sign of any kind of brain trauma yet to warrant operating on. The operation would be close to half a million dollars with his insurance, a fact that did not escape the hospital administrators, nor Walter. While he was admittedly worried about making things worse for his son, as his medical proxy he was steadfast in his decision to not let the doctors operate on him.

The doctors still routinely offered, and Ronnie wanted to make sure his parents didn't cave to their pressure, because she also had faith in him. He had promised to fight for their love, and this was his first test.

"Have his parents come by today?"

"Not yet, but I'm sure they'll be coming soon. I got you an apple juice and the graham crackers you like."

Ronnie's green eyes lit up. It was another minor victory. "Is it sad that I've been looking forward to these all day?" she smirked.

"Well, it's a good thing I got you two packs."

The graham crackers were one of the hospital treats that she adored. They had the right amount of sugar and cinnamon. She'd even looked in several stores for the same brand but couldn't find them. Within these walls, they were currency.

Ronnie snatched the pack out of his hand like a kid opening a

Christmas present. She took a bite of one and relished the taste of the cinnamon and sugar sprinkles on her tongue. She closed her eyes in elation.

After a second bite, she glanced at the nurse, her hero of the night. "Jacob, I'm glad to have met you. I wish the circumstances were different, of course."

"Thank you, Mrs.... I mean, Ronnie. I'll give you time alone with him now."

She was lying. In fact, she hated that she'd ever met Jacob. She hated that she was even in this hospital. She wanted to leave and never talk to any of these people again, but as long as her lover was here, she'd be here.

As Jacob walked out the door, Ronnie placed the crackers on a counter and changed clothes. She had a black and pink Nike t-shirt that read, "Strike fear or get struck," as well as her black spandex tights. As she changed, she unfolded the events of the day to Lucas, like she'd been doing every visit.

"Well, this week has been no better than the last. Your mother is in Psalms, so I'd say about halfway through the bible. She reads aloud every day she's here, which I wouldn't care about at all if I could take an Ambien. But because I'm now a baby momma – temporarily, anyway – I have to listen to more 'thee's and 'thou's than I've heard since I was a damn kid. Sometimes I wish you'd just jump up and say, 'I'm alive, praise the Lord!' It would scare her shitless, I'm sure. Of course, that means we'd probably be in church for the rest of our lives because of that miracle, and I don't know if I could stand church for three hours."

She checked her work emails as she continued. "As far as work goes, Nichelle still isn't returning anyone's calls – at least not mine, the worthless wench. The city is still on fire because of your shooting. You could solve a lot of this by waking up, you know.

"The good news is, I hired you the best lawyer in the city, who tells me this is almost a slam dunk of a civil case, considering the climate of the nation and the circumstances. She literally climaxes at the thought of winning a multi-million-dollar payday. So, whether they find this asshole guilty or not, it's safe to say you'll be a rich man when you wake up and we get back to our lives. Good thing too, because you're going to spend a small fortune on the wedding. 'Course, you probably already knew that, but after what you're putting me through right now, I'm more than worth it. We'll just have to deal with Nichelle's jealousy, which will only make it that much more enjoyable... I should make her a bridesmaid."

She laughed at the idea. Then took a sigh and said.

"I'm sure we haven't heard the last of that heifer. She's probably plotting right now on her leave of absence. I mean, to even think about taking a leave of absence now. It's absurd, and so now I'm stuck doing her job and mine, which is bullshit." Ronnie stroked the keyboard to reply to an email and then continued.

"Now I know what you're going to say, and the answer is yes. Technically, this is what I wanted all along, but only after the promotion. Now I'm just bringing down my billing rate, and to make matters worse, they're considering bringing back Kendra. You don't know her, but she's the girl they transferred to make space for Nichelle. It's just frustrating, because you're my fiancé, yet she gets to take leave because they shot you in her house? Honestly, Lucas, I don't know what you ever saw in her. She is manipulative, selfish, and tasteless. I have my own list of sins, but at least I dress well."

She took another bite of the graham cracker and continued through her chewing. "And before you go defending her, let me note this: Nichelle was tacky on a good day. I mean, she had a few cute outfits here and there, but her hair was never right when she wore it natural, or whatever you want to call what she was doing to her head. She kept trying to highlight her big ass, as if we were on some reality TV show on basic cable."

Ronnie moved to sit on the edge of her lover's bed.

"You need to wake up, baby." She rubbed his cheek. "There's so much we need to talk about, so much I need to apologize for, even now. Lucas, if you can hear me, I know I say this every day, but I really do regret my last words to you. And I don't know if you'll forgive me for my words or my decisions, but I'll live with that. I liked who I was becoming with you, and I want to keep going. I'll be more transparent, and I'll never ever speak so harshly to you again. Hell, I'll even learn to like Nichelle if you would just wake the fuck up."

Beep. Beep. Beep.

The concert went on.

2
WORSER

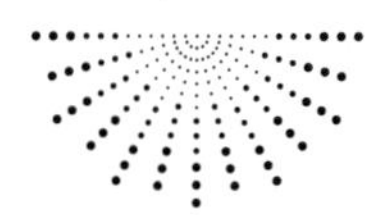

"Your dandelions need watering," she noted as she straightened up the room. She got a cup of water and fed them. "You'd be surprised at how much these little flowers consume. The hospital had a fit about me keeping these in here, but your dad had my back on this one."

She walked back towards him, taking in his appearance. The definition in his jawline was softening. He was losing muscle, and it had only been a few weeks. It would have been unnoticeable to someone who didn't know him intimately, but the longer he stayed in his comatose state, the more she paid attention to the details of her would-be groom.

"You did all of this, you know. I was just going to get some coffee one day, and there your charming ass was, wearing the hell out of that Oscar de la Renta suit. And now I'm pregnant. Why the hell did I stop to ask if you were okay? It was that damn suit! The way your chest popped in it, and those puppy dog eyes, you looked too good not to say hello to. I was just fine being Ronnie. No chinks in my armor. Now I'm here talking to myself, getting water for these damn flowers, for a man who can't even see them. I guess good dick will do that to you. Well, that and a Tiffany's box." She smirked as she looked at her engagement ring in all its splendor.

"I'll be right back." She leaned in and kissed him gently on the cheek before proceeding into the hallway.

As she opened the door, she turned and bumped into a man whose Calvin Klein scent was unmistakable. "Walter, I'm sorry, I didn't see you there." Ronnie said to Lucas' father.

"You never need to apologize to me, darlin'," the older gentleman replied. "Going out to get some water for those little flowers you guys like so much, I see."

"You know it."

"What's the deal with the dandelions?"

"Excuse me?"

"Every week since we've been here, you've brought dandelions to his room at the start of the week. I heard you say to the nurse you want them to be the first thing he sees when he wakes up, but the gardener in me just has to know: why dandelions?"

"I'm not sure what you mean," Ronnie replied.

"It's an unusual flower, a weed around these parts. So, what's the deal with dandelions between you two?"

Ronnie smiled. She could go into how she and his son used it as a safe-word for their sexual escapades – and if it were Lucas' mother asking, she very well would have – but she liked Walter, and talking to him made her feel like she was talking to Lucas in a way, so she spared him the details. "It was the first flower he ever gave me."

"To a woman as pretty as you? Now I taught the boy better than that. He knows darn good and well those are weeds."

"You did a good job, Walter. Before I met him, I didn't know that they'd become something more than the little flakes we blow away in the spring. I think it was his way of showing he sees the beauty in everything, even the unlovable."

"Now that makes sense. The boy always did – *does* – things with meaning. And to be clear, you aren't unlovable. Well, no sense in you walking all the way down the hall. Use this." He handed her a water bottle, one of several he had in the satchel he typically carried when visiting his son.

She smiled and took the water. "Thank you, Walter."

"Anytime, sweetheart. Now tell me, how are you doing?" he asked as they proceeded back into the room.

"Well, you can't fall off the floor, so there's nowhere to go but up," she said in a moment of vulnerability.

Walter pulled her into his arms. "He's going to be okay, you know that, right?"

"I don't know, Walt—"

"Luke will be fine. The gunshot wound is the worst of it. Hell, he's had worse injuries from roughhousing with his brothers. He'll be back in no time, you hear me?"

"It's hard to believe right now, but I'll believe because you do."

"And I'm not worried one bit."

She held him a little tighter. She liked Walter. It was more than just that he was Lucas' father; she really liked him as a person. He had a warm nature that settled her. He even ignored the fact that she was strongly considering terminating his unborn grandchild. She'd promised herself she wouldn't lie to him.

"How's our other boy?" Walter enquired, as if reading her thoughts.

She removed herself from the embrace. "Walter… look, I—"

"Now, I know you haven't decided, and I'm not trying to pressure you, it's just that with everything going on, it's a bright spot for me right now, that's all."

Ronnie wasn't sure what to say. Before the incident, she'd been dead set against having children, and she couldn't be pressured into it. Still, with each passing day, a decision would have to be made.

She looked at Walter. "I'm pretty sure it's a girl."

She caught a giant grin out of the corner of her eye. "That's fine. I'll teach her how to root for those Texans."

"She won't watch sports, Walter."

"Come on, Ronnie, you know if he or she's gonna be a Kimble, she's gonna be spending her Sundays either at church or watching football."

"Hmmm, you have a point. Go Texans, I guess?" she said uncertainly.

The pair laughed at her words. Ronnie glanced at Lucas then back at Walter and said.

"Speaking of church, where is Natalie?"

"Thursday is her night to meet with the prayer warriors. They pray for Lucas for an hour and then she comes to the hospital."

"Oh, that's right."

"But she won't be coming tonight. She's going home. The same place I'm sending you."

Ronnie, still standing, defended herself. "Walter, I'm fine."

"Listen, Ronnie, you've been here every night, and right now there's not a lot anyone but God can do for him. I'm sure there are things you need to do that you can't do here. Go home, eat some good food, and get a good night's rest. Get away from this place. If anything happens, I'll call and let you know."

"Walter, I'm really fine."

"You might be okay, but I'm not taking no for an answer. You and that baby need a proper night's sleep in an actual bed. Besides, I have a few things I gotta talk to my son about, man to man. Go home, Ronnie."

It was the most direct he'd ever been with her in the time they'd known each other. Maybe he was tired of being strong and didn't want her to see him vulnerable, or he just wanted to spend some time with his son. In either case, Ronnie took the hint and gave him one last hug before gathering her belongings.

Walter was right – she could use a good night's sleep, and there wasn't much she could do here.

One night away's not going to hurt.

She nodded and grabbed her keys, turning to Walter. "Call me—"

"If anything changes, I'll call you first and Natalie second."

She smiled and walked towards the elevators. Her misfortune had a slight reprieve, if only for one day.

Suspicious – going to pull the plug while they are both gone? Its been 3 wks

"It's just one night," she mumbled to herself.

She wanted to be next to Lucas; even in this state, being next to him was more comforting than being without him.

She left the hospital and had made it to the parking lot when she heard a familiar voice call her name. "Ms. Duvalle?"

She turned to see Officer Santiago, the man who'd shot Lucas.

She glared at the man. "You have a lot of fucking nerve—"

"Please, I just… I know I shouldn't be here, but I needed to talk to you."

She looked him over. It was difficult to compare the man standing in front of her with the picture that had been circulating on the news, because she could see his defeated spirit. She could tell he'd been drinking.

"What do you want?" she asked reluctantly.

"The shooting…I…I was just doing my job, Ms. Duvalle. I'm a good cop, and I was just doing my job. I didn't do anything wrong."

"If that were true, we wouldn't be having this conversation in the parking lot of a hospital, now would we?"

"What do you want, Ms. Duvalle? Do you want an apology? Your lawyer… she's digging up everything I've ever done and twisting it."

"Oh, like your previous assault on a defenseless man?"

"That happened when I was a kid. I wasn't even on the force then. I was drunk, fighting over a girl who is now my wife. We have three kids now. My pension, everything I work for, is for them. Please, Ms. Duvalle, I'm asking – no, I'm begging you – to stop this. I can't afford the legal fees. I just want to be a cop again. She's ruining my life."

"You're groveling, that's good. But, she's just getting started, because I'm just getting started. Let me ask you a question. Do you like the heels on these shoes?"

"Ms. Duvalle I—"

"I ask because I want you to remember them. I'm going to crush you under my heel, and once you've lost everything, that's when I'll really lean on you. By the time I'm done, you're going to wish it was me you shot in that apartment. You want this to end? The only way that happens is with you on your knees, kissing the soles of my feet, begging me to stop. Now, unless you want to compound your legal woes with a harassment case, I suggest you take your doughnut eating ass somewhere else."

She turned around and walked away from the officer, delighting at the sight of the man in ruin. The city wanted this to go away fast, and judging by Officer Santiago's desperation to seek her out, he was certainly feeling the pressure.

She pushed the conversation to the back of her mind and pulled out her cell phone, which had been vibrating while she was talking to the cop. There were several missed calls: one from Kendra, and the rest from a number whose area code she knew all too well. "337," she murmured aloud.

Her stomach sank. She was irate at the sight of this area code on her phone. Ronnie opened the settings to block the number as the phone rang again. In her haste, she mistakenly answered the call, which she instantly regretted. She could already hear a female voice with a strong creole twang on the other end of the phone.

"Ronnie? Can you hear me?"

"Hey, Rue."

"We need to talk."

3
THESE ARE THE DAYS

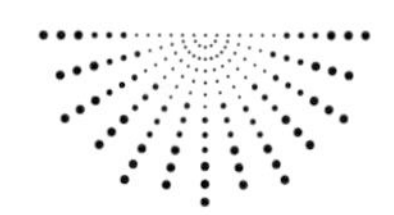

"Well, try not to sound too excited," Valerie Duvalle said to her sister Ronnie.

"Rue, I'm—"

"Busy, I know. You're always busy, and then shortly thereafter the phone seems to infinitely go to voicemail. What are the odds?"

"I don't know what you're talking about."

"Of course you don't."

"Rue, believe what you want, but I'm walking into a meeting right now."

"At this hour? I'm sure you are."

"You know, some of us have to work, not sit at home catering to a man all da—"

"Malcolm died." Oop!

The words stunned her. She liked her sister's husband, and normally this would've been upsetting, but it was one more emotional log on an already-roaring fire. She couldn't contain it any longer. She muted the phone and sobbed openly –her pride wouldn't allow her the satisfaction of letting her sister hear her sob.

As she composed herself, she could hear her sister Rue say, "Ronnie, did you hear me?"

"I did. I'm sorry for your loss. I always liked Malcolm," she said.

"Well, thank you. It's not just my loss, Ronnie. Despite what you think, Malcolm always thought of you as family."

"I didn't mean it like that. I…look, that sounded insensitive, but there's just a lot of shit going on right now. I respected Malcolm. He was a good man. Can I ask what happened?"

"Well, we haven't talked in a while, so you didn't know that he'd been fighting ALS for some time now. Over the last year, it got more aggressive. The doctors insisted he stay at a hospice, but you know Malcolm; he just wanted to live in his own home, and so he died here."

Ronnie was silent.

"Ronnie? You still there?"

"I'm…what? I didn't know he was that sick." She was stunned by the news.

"I think this is one of those conversations we need to have in person. Besides, Malcolm would want you to be here. He made it very clear: it's time for you to come home."

"Rue, like I said, I got a lot going on here."

"Oh, I'm sure there's a ton. Which is why you've been ducking calls for the last God knows how many years now. Don't you think I've had a lot going on? Look, Malcolm made me promise that you'd be at his funeral, and though he'd never say that you owed him anything, we both know you do."

Ronnie paused. She wanted to hang up, but she couldn't. Before she'd met Lucas, Malcolm was the nicest man she'd ever met. He was the reason she'd been able to leave Breaux Bridge, Louisiana, by funding her education.

"How are you doing with it all?"

"I'm glad it's over. It was rough."

"I can imagine, between dealing with him *and* her."

"And by 'her', I'm assuming you mean momma. She wasn't invited, and I don't think she's going to come. 'Get rid of all bitterness, rage and anger, brawling and slander, along with every form of malice. Be kind and compassionate to one another, forgiving each other, just as in Christ God forgave you.'"

"Ephesians 4:31 and 32," Ronnie replied.

"I didn't think you'd remember that."

"It's hard to forget, Rue. Besides, I met a lady who reads the bible chapter by chapter every day, and we've already covered Ephesians."

The pair laughed.

"Look, *chile,* it's been too long. You might feel like there's nothing here for you, and maybe there ain't, but the only way you can find out is if you come home."

"I'll see what I can do."

"You're a Duvalle. Don't see what you can do. Just *do*."

Ronnie took a deep breath and rolled her eyes. "Bye, Rue."

4

THE ART OF THE DEAL

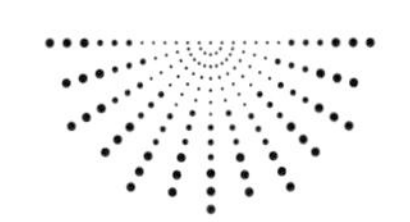

Ronnie hung up the phone in frustration. She put the phone back in her purse and scrubbed her hands across her face, as if to wipe away the emotions that had come with the conversation. She hadn't heard from her sister in years, mostly because she'd done her best to avoid her and Breaux Bridge, Louisiana. In some ways, the call was a welcome relief from her constant worrying about Lucas and whether she should keep the baby.

Ronnie finally left the hospital, looking forward to sleeping in her own bed.

She was halfway home when the phone rang again. This time she checked the Bluetooth screen to make sure it wasn't her sister.

The screen lit up with the name Basic Bitch, along with the accompanying photo of Kendra Daniels, her frenemy that was becoming an ever-growing problem.

She took a deep breath and answered the phone yet again, rolling her eyes. "Diva, what's going on?" she asked, her voice as warm and bubbly as she could muster.

"Hoe, what you doing?"

"I'm leaving the hospital. What about you? Just finished sucking dick?"

"Two, in fact."

"Light day for you, then."

The two chuckled for a moment. "Well, it's official! Ya girl is coming back to Houston!"

"That's... incredible news."

Ronnie tried to keep the anger out of her tone. She slammed her hand against the console but wasn't quiet enough.

"What was that noise?"

"Huh? Oh, some dumbass tried to get over on the road," she replied.

"Oh, that's one thing I'm not looking forward to, the bad driving. But back to me. It's going to be good to have some more black girl magic in the sausage factory. Maybe we can be on the same team this time around?"

"Girl, say no more."

"I know you got my back."

"So, I guess things are over with Marcus for real now?"

"Fuck Marcus Winters. I'll tell you all about it when I see you."

"See me?"

"Oh, I didn't mention? I should be there in the next week or two. I have nothing tying me down here, so it's just about finding a place to live."

"Wonderful," Ronnie said as she sped past the exit to her condo. Suddenly, she wasn't in the mood to head home anymore.

"Well, if you need a place to stay until you figure it out, I have more than enough space at my place."

"Ronnie, you'd do that for me?"

"Kendra, since when have I not looked out for you? You're my girl. Anything you need, I've got you covered."

"Aww, you're such a thoughtful bitch when you wanna be. I might take you up on that. But first I have to see if I can work things out with the guy I met."

"Let the record state that you jumped off one dick to ride a brand new one."

"Ronnie."

"I'm just saying, let the walls heal first, girl." They both laughed as Ronnie reached her new destination. "Okay, girlfriend, I have to get off the phone. I have some business I need to handle."

"You going out to drink?"

"No, this is work stuff. It shouldn't take long."

"Okay, call me back when you get free."

"Will do. Bye."

She hung up the phone and parked the car, looking across the street to the three-story home in the heart of River Oaks.

Exiting the car, she walked up the entry steps and rang the doorbell multiple times. The door opened and a middle-aged, dark-haired Hispanic woman greeted her.

"Hi, you must be the housekeeper. Nice to meet you. I'm the help. Excuse me."

Ronnie barged her way into the foyer.

A tall, perky blonde woman, who instantly reminded Ronnie of Nicole Kidman in *The Stepford Wives,* came to investigate the interruption.

We love our appearances, don't we? She thought.

This was exactly the type of woman Milton would marry for the sake of the company's image.

"Excuse me, miss, are you lost? Can I help you?"

"Yes, you can. You must be Jenna."

"I am, and you are?"

"Well, that depends. At the moment, I'm vice president of Burrows Industries but one way or another, my title as far as you're concerned, is about to change."

"I'm sorry, I'm not following."

"I'm sure that's a common occurrence for you. Don't strain your brain. I'm here to see your husband, Jenna."

As she finished, Milton Burrows walked into the room, bellowing, "Honey, who is at the—oh my damn."

Ronnie turned to see Milton, his eyes widening at her presence. He loosened his burgundy tie as he hurried down the stairs.

"Well, there he is, the CE-motherfucking-O. We need to talk."

Ronnie smirked as he visibly turned red. He stormed toward her and she folded her arms, giving him pause. She watched as Milton looked over at his wife, Jenna, who was clearly expecting some sort of explanation.

"Milton, who is this woman, and why is she in our home?" the woman asked.

"Honey, it's a work issue. It won't take very long."

Ronnie glanced over at the housekeeper, who seemed well-aware of the situation. The two made eye contact and Ronnie, with a twitch of her eyebrow, asked if Jenna was aware of her husband's extracurricular activities. The maid gave a subtle shake of her head, to which Ronnie winked in acknowledgment.

Milton stormed past the both of them to open the door, motioning Ronnie outside. Ronnie stood still as Milton opened the door. "Ms. Duvalle, can we please step outside?"

"I'm comfortable right here. Besides, I'm sure that anything I can say to you, I can say in front of your lovely wife."

"That's true, but...I...please, it would be better for us to talk in private."

Ronnie walked towards the door. As she reached the threshold, she turned to address Jenna, who looked confused about the whole exchange. "It was nice to finally meet you, Jenna. I'm sure we'll be in touch again soon."

As she stepped outside, her faux smile quickly transformed into a bristling snarl. "You lying, backstabbing, son of a bitch! You brought Kendra Daniels down here to replace Nichelle?"

"Ronnie, please calm down."

"I will do no such thing, you two-faced motherfucker. We had a deal."

"You don't understand."

"What don't I understand? That Kendra Daniels is replacing Nichelle, or that you've allowed Nichelle a leave of absence for no logical reason I can think of, or for stiffing me with her work in the process?"

Milton nervously looked around to see if anyone on the street was watching. "Ronnie, believe me, I—"

"Let me tell you what I don't understand. I don't understand how, after making the shareholders millions of dollars, you thought you could sidestep me yet again. Where the fuck is my promotion? Help me understand, Milton, before I teach Jenna how property laws work in the state of Texas."

"Ronnie, this is not my doing. The board—"

"You know what, Milton? I'm getting real sick of this shit about the board. Are you the CEO or a fucking Walmart employee?"

"It's not that simple. I ha—"

"If you can't make it that simple, then it must be the latter, and since you clearly can't get shit done, I need to speak to your supervisor."

"What do you mean, my supervisor?"

"I want a meeting with the board, since you don't have the scrotum for such a basic task."

Milton was just about to respond when the door opened, and Jenna walked out to join the conversation. "I'm sorry to interrupt y'all, but is everything okay?"

Ronnie looked at Milton, who looked as if he were a deer in the headlights. "Well, Jenna, I think we've come to an agreement. I'm so sorry to come over like this. Please enjoy your family time. Milton, I'll see you at 9 a.m. sharp in the Navaho Conference Room for our meeting with the board?" she asked.

"R...right, 9 o'clock."

"Excellent. I'll see you then."

5
LUST AND DESIRE

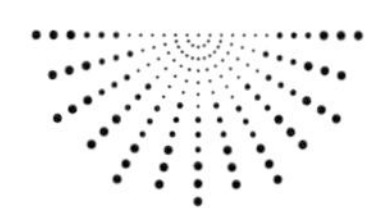

Ronnie woke up the next morning energized for her upcoming meeting. She was slightly on edge, and wasn't sure why. She was about to get out of bed when it dawned on her.

"I need some dick right now, Lord."

Her fingers moving to her clit. As she began massaging it, one of her fingers found its way to her pussy, and it's warm moisture saturated her fingers.

"Damn it! I can't go to work like this," she muttered.

She reached over to the top drawer of her nightstand and pulled out her vibrator, placing it inside her pulsating pussy. As it slid in and she turned it on, all she could think about was Lucas and their last time together.

She recalled waking up, and the way he'd dominated her, physically and emotionally. She yearned to feel his thick dick inside of her.

"Damnit, I miss you, Luke," she whispered at the memory of sweat dripping from his hardened chest as he thrust inside of her.

Ronnie turned up the intensity on her vibrator.

The wetter she got, the more real it all felt; his tongue ravishing her pussy with the reckless abandon she needed. It was as if he was there inside of her, whispering in her ear, *I love you.*

"I'm cumming," she moaned as the pleasure erupted through her body, her fluids saturating the vibrator.

But her mind wasn't ready to leave him yet. She wanted more. "Stay with me, baby," she moaned.

She cast her mind back to the first time he'd made love to her; the slapping against her ass cheeks when the fullness of his nine-and-a-half-inch dick was inside of her, the curve of his manhood, and how the bulging vein rubbed perfectly against her g-spot; his sweet nectar warming her insides as he huffed heavily, drenched in sweat from each masterful thrust.

"That's it. Fuck me, daddy."

Ronnie rolled her eyes as another orgasm flowed through her.

When she regained her composure, she looked at her soaked sheets. "Clean up on aisle three," she joked.

She tried to get up, but right now she couldn't move; she was still coming down from her high.

"Damn, baby, I miss you."

He meant the world to her, but the world would have to wait.

After a few deep breaths, she got up and cleaned up for the day. She tried to pick out an outfit for the meeting but couldn't make up her mind. She considered calling Kendra because, although she had terrible choices in men, they had similar styles.

Ronnie picked out a blue dress and pressed it against her, trying to imagine the entire outfit, then did the same with a black one.

She took a picture of both and sent it to Kendra.

Which one?

In moments, she got a response. *The black one.*

"Alpha bitch it is," she said, looking down at her still-flat stomach.

Putting on a black jacket over her dress, she gave herself a once-over in the full-length mirror before sending another picture to Kendra.

Looks like an alpha bitch day at the office.

She chuckled, and then suddenly felt queasy. "Damnit, don't do this to me now!" she grumbled. "This is an important day, and if you mess this up..."

She caught herself in the full-sized mirror wagging her finger at the baby.

Girl, what are you doing?

She'd found herself talking to the baby more and more lately. It had become a source of comfort since Lucas wasn't around, but the more she visited the hospital, the more she began to doubt everything.

What if Lucas never woke up? She thought.

She'd missed her previous appointment with Planned Parenthood because of recent events, but nothing was stopping her from rebooking – nothing other than her promise to Lucas that she would think about keeping it, and that she wasn't alone.

I don't have time to think about this now. Get it together.

As she headed out the door, a bout of morning sickness hit. She hurried to the restroom, scrambling to the toilet, but she was too late.

Her stomach emptied itself, most of it hitting the toilet, but some hit her dress and shoes.

Finally the upending came to an end, and she wiped her sleeve across her mouth. "Damnit! I cannot do nine months of this shit! If you're gonna be in there, you can't be annoying," she admonished her stomach, somewhat in jest.

Quickly changing her outfit to the blue dress, she left the house.

It was time to get the promotion she'd earned.

Her drive wasn't long to work, and she was eager to arrive. If Milton took her threat seriously, the board should be in the conference room today, and that meant she was in for a battle. She knew it would take some convincing; this was a company not adept with change, but they did all agree on one thing: money, and she brought that in hand over fist. Right now, with their stock being at an all-time high – thanks to her direction – she was in the driver's seat.

Strike while the iron's hot. It's my time.

It wasn't long before she was in her private parking space and walking into the building. She was fully prepared to fight for the position, with every counter-argument for her promotion already prepared in her mind. By the time she cleared security, she was certain there was nothing they could throw at her that would catch her by surprise.

There was an air of confidence in her as she thought about it all. Despite Lucas being shot, taking on Nichelle's work, and Kendra coming back to compete against her, she was at the top of her game, and nothing could hinder her plan. Today she would put Burrows Industries on notice about their best talent.

As she got off the elevator and headed toward the boardroom, a calmness set in.

This is my time.

She repeated in her head. When she opened the door, she felt nauseous again – this time induced by the empty boardroom.

I know this motherfucker didn't just test me!

Milton was a lot of things; at the top of the list was a coward. There was no way he would call her bluff, especially since she wasn't bluffing.

The clock on the wall showed it was 8:52. There should be food or coffee set up in the room by now. Instead, there was silence, and the lights were off.

No, there would be no meeting today.

Okay, Milton, we'll play it your way.

Ronnie took a deep breath and stormed towards her office.

It was time to rain hell on Milton Burrows.

She was halfway to the elevator when Milton came around the corner.

With composure, she charged him. "Milton, can you explain to me what the fuck I've made unclear about today?"

Milton, already red, as if he were expecting the humiliation, responded in a very sheepish tone, "Ronnie, please just listen to me."

"The time for words has come and gone, Milton. The amount of restraint I've shown is biblical. I have —"

"For the love of God, will you just let me explain? Please?"

"There is nothing to explain. I made myself clear last night, and apparently you think this is a poker game. Well, the stakes are high, bitch, and I'm all in."

She pulled out her phone to dial a number when another man rounded the corner.

"So, you must be the goose that laid the golden egg. You've made us all very wealthy in the last few days."

Two security guards hovered behind him. There was no question who was standing in front of her – his picture was all over the building.

It was suddenly clear why she didn't get her promotion. Martin Burrows, Milton's father and the founder of Burrows Industries, rarely appeared at the firm, but he'd made the time today.

6
DANGEROUS LIAISONS

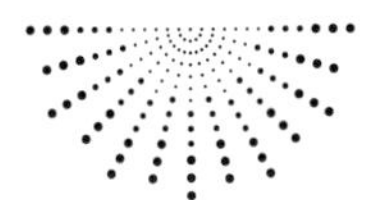

"Milton, introduce me," he ordered.

Ronnie looked to Milton, who had all the confidence of a sixth grader who'd failed his geometry test. "Ronnie Duvalle, my father, Martin Burrows. He'd like to speak with you."

Ronnie examined the man. He stood at five-feet-ten, with silver hair that was balding. He wore a black peacoat that covered a charcoal suit with a solid blue tie. Everything about him was how she'd imagined it. He was old money.

"It's nice to finally meet you." Ronnie said. She felt the urge to throw up, but she fought to restrain it.

"Likewise, Ms. Duvalle. Let's take a walk."

Ronnie glanced at Milton, who quickly looked away.

She nodded at Martin.

"David will hold on to your belongings, to make sure nothing happens to them."

Ronnie looked over at the security guard, a six-foot-five stocky black man with piercing eyes. By the looks of him, she doubted she had a choice in the matter. She handed her purse to the security guard as he escorted the two of them to the private elevator.

Ronnie looked back at Milton, who wouldn't make eye contact with either of them. His father must have berated him at some point.

Daddy issues-having motherfucker.

The trip in the elevator was a first for her – only Martin had access. She hadn't even been sure it worked, but the elevator took them directly from the top floor to the basement, where Martin's driver was waiting.

David opened the rear door of a black late-model Lincoln Navigator, motioning for her to go in first.

So, this is how old money rolls.

As impressive as the car was, there was an air of uneasiness inside. She wasn't sure what was going to happen, or why Martin Burrows had given her his personal attention, but she knew there was a problem.

Let's see how this plays out. She thought as silence filled the air.

"Crazy weather we're having, isn't it?" he said to break the ice.

She looked out the window. "It's Houston. Each day is as unpredictable as the next. But I'm sure you didn't call me down here to take a drive in this lovely car and talk about the weather."

"You're direct. I can see why Milton likes you," Martin responded with a chuckle.

"So, I have to ask: why am I here? Promotions aren't usually given in the back seat of a Lincoln Navigator."

Martin laughed again. "You've got a lot of spunk for one of your kind."

"And what kind would that be, Martin? A woman, or a person of color?" Ronnie challenged.

"Both."

She gritted her teeth, but the response didn't surprise her. It was why Martin didn't want phones in the car.

Martin ignored her reaction. "When I was a child, my father got me a collie. Her name was Lizzie. She looked just like Lassie. I loved that dog. We had a bond like any boy and dog should have. But my pa couldn't stand her. She had a habit of eating apples straight from the tree, and it was my job to keep her from getting in the apples. To make things worse, the damn dog would have diarrhea after eating them."

Martin took a sip of water and continued. "One day, my dad told me to take her to the apple tree and let her eat as many apples as she wanted, making sure to count them. She had a marvelous time, and I enjoyed watching her." Ronnie nodded and sat silent as he continued.

"Well, when she was about done feasting, my dad came outside and in his hand was a newspaper. He asked me how many apples she had eaten, and I said eleven. He rolled up the newspaper and told me to hit her as hard as I could across the nose with the newspaper eleven times.

"I was stunned. Like I said, Lizzie was never any real trouble, and I didn't want to harm her, but my father insisted. 'You hit her or I hit you. It's your call.' So, I took the newspaper and belted my Lizzie across the nose eleven times. By the sixth time, her nose was bleeding and I was crying. When I was done, the tip of the newspaper was drenched in Lizzie's blood. When I let her go, she yelped and ran off. I had hurt my best friend." There was a chill in the air. Martin glanced out the window and continued his story.

"My pa put his arm around my shoulders and said, 'Son, you could've kept cleaning up that dog's shit every time she got into the apples, but what you did today made sure she'll never bother the apples again. Sometimes you just have to put a bitch in her place.'"

It was cold, but his message was simple: she was not getting a promotion anytime soon.

Ronnie nodded. "Well, it's a good thing we got rid of those pesky phones, because if anyone were to hear what such a well-known philanthropist was saying, well...it wouldn't be pretty."

"I know what you're thinking. Martin Burrows is sexist, or racist. But what is truly important to note is, I don't give a shit what you think. The reality is, my name is the one on the goddamn building, so I can be or say anything I goddamn please. You think because my son can't keep it in his pants, that earns you a seat at the table? My table? Let me be clear: as long as you work for my firm, I make the rules. Move on from this promotion business."

Ronnie looked at her employer. He'd shown his true colors, yet none of it shocked her. She smirked and then asked. "You know, they say every great empire has been built on a crime. I wonder, Martin, what crimes have you committed in pursuit of your empire?"

There was a brief silence as Martin gazed out of the window at the passing city, as if to process her comment. After a spell, Martin responded. "Look around, Ms. Duvalle. A fresh wave is coming, and you're on the wrong side of the tide. The days of affirmative action, placing unqualified workers in positions for appearance's sake, are over. It's time this country lived up to its creed."

"Oh, I see. You want to make it great again?" —Trump

"People think that money brings fewer problems. That's absolutely false. What it does buy, however, is the luxury to not worry about your problems. Take this… dilemma with you, for instance. Now, you could either take what is going to be a very generous bonus check for all your hard work and go back to doing the job we are paying you handsomely for, and all will be right with the world, or I could take that same amount of coin and deal with this another way. Either way, the issue with you will be buried." threat!

Ronnie was silent.

Every empire was built on a crime, and Martin had all but confessed that no crime was off the table. *You will be buried* may have meant he would end her career, or it could be literal.

A jolt of fear shot through her system like lightning. Martin cut his eyes at her and asked.

"So…have we come to an understanding?"

"Crystal clear. I don't want no trouble, boss." Ronnie said sarcastically.

Martin smirked, appreciating her tone.

As the car pulled up to the office building, Martin said, "One last thing. Don't show up at my son's house unannounced ever again. This foolishness between you and him ends now."

now she gotta kill the boss

7
BETRAYAL AND REVENGE

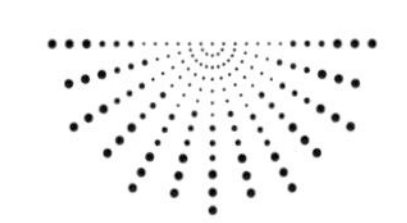

Milton approached the car as it pulled into the building's lot, looking at her with the same shame and embarrassment he had earlier. She collected her things from the bodyguard, and hastily dashed inside.

She walked into the first women's restroom she could find and threw up.

Tears flowed freely down her cheeks. She wasn't sure if it was the emotion from the encounter, the baby's hormones, or the fact that she once again was denied the promotion she so desperately worked for.

"Son of a bitch!" she yelled, as she sobbed heavily in the bathroom stall. After a few minutes, she pulled herself together, took several breaths, and stepped outside to freshen up.

When she got back to her office, she sat quietly, thinking about Martin's not-so-veiled threat. There was a chill in her spirit that moved through her like a cool, fall wind before a cold front.

By noon, she'd decided she'd had enough. Her phone showed she'd missed three calls from her sister.

Malcolm's funeral. You know what, fuck this place.

Ronnie got on her computer and drafted an email to her department heads, making sure Milton was copied on the email.

Hi team,

Effective immediately, I will be on vacation. You can reach me on my cell.

Ronnie

As she tapped the last word, she hovered the mouse over the 'Send' button and hesitated.

Those seventeen words meant failure. She'd never taken a vacation, but it was all getting to be too much.

As she was about to hit send, her assistant Doug, walked in. "Ms. Duvalle, is everything okay?"

"I'm fine, Doug, just about to leave on vacation. What do you want?"

"Someone…well, I think it was a bodyguard, just dropped off a package for you from Mr. Burrows. Not Mr. Burrows, the CEO, but his father. He said you would understand."

Ronnie got up from her desk and took the package from Doug, who lingered long enough to inspect what it was.

In the box contained a rolled-up copy of today's Houston Chronicle, the city's local newspaper. She took the newspaper out and threw it in the trash.

Oh, I got your bitch. She thought.

She walked over to her desk and sent the email.

She looked at the newspaper sitting in her trashcan and her mood turned malevolent. As she brewed in her own thoughts, she realized that Doug still stood in her office.

"Something you need, Doug?" she barked at him. She could tell he had something on his mind he needed to express. She watched as he squirmed, mustering up the courage to ask about the only thing that could matter to him: the rumors of layoffs. In the mood she was in, she had no problem taking her frustrations out on him.

"I wanted to see if you were okay," he finally said.

"I'm fine."

"It's just that, you're going on vacation and…well, you've never taken one… at least not since I've been here."

"Doug, is there a question at the end of this airstrip, or are you just taking your sweet time landing the plane because you enjoy my company?" He tensed up. She could tell he was about to turn around and walk to his desk. "Speak your mind, Douglas."

"Ms. Duvalle, you know I'd do anything for you...I just want to know, people are talking about—"

"You're wasting my time. Now, ask me a direct question if you want a direct answer."

The man in front of her tugged at his collar, stammering over his words. She knew he wanted to know about the layoffs. Were the rumors true and, more importantly, was he on the list? He wanted reassurance and would find none from her. Layoffs were imminent, and Doug was on the list as her personal sacrifice for a job she would no longer get.

She wanted to unload her entire plan on him, from conception to completion, and how he'd been collateral damage in her quest for power. She wanted to see him become enraged so she could berate him, deserving or not. A confrontation was what she wanted.

As she realized Doug would be an unwitting target of her fury, he spoke. "I just wanted to know—"

"One second, Doug."

Her cell was ringing from her desk — Rue again. Her sister wouldn't stop calling until she got what she wanted, a trait they both shared. She glanced again at the newspaper sitting in the waste bucket next to her desk.

I need to get out of here.

The funeral was the perfect opportunity to regroup.

"Ms. Duvalle, I know your time is valuable. Is everything okay?"

"No, it's not Doug. The rumors are true; there will be layoffs coming. And I've been in such a foul mood because they want me to terminate you."

He slumped over, devastated by the news. He looked shattered, and she wanted him to fester in it.

"Listen to me, Doug. I will not let that happen. I know I can be a lot, but you're the best assistant in this goddamn office, and I've been fighting tooth and nail to keep you around."

It was all a lie; she'd made a point of making him the sacrificial lamb weeks ago in front of the board, for all to see. But with Martin tipping the scale she realized there was no reason to throw away a pawn this early into the game.

She watched as he tried to rationalize what had happened. “But I don’t understand why—”

“It’s a numbers game, Douglas. I tried to keep you around, maybe partner you with Kendra Daniels or another executive, but they just wouldn’t budge. I have an idea though. I’m gonna fight for your job. You just have to trust me, and only me, because we’re in this together.”

“Ms. Duvalle, please help me. I have student loans, and I like working for you.”

“I know. Don’t worry, you’ll be working for me as long as I’m at this firm. But there are a few things we have to do first. Right now, I need to be with my sister. Her husband just died. I’m taking personal time to be with my family.”

“Oh goodness! I’m so sorry to hear that. Is she okay?”

“No, she’s not – hell, I’m not. We’re all taking it pretty hard, which is why I’m taking leave. Please don’t tell anyone, but I’m going to be gone a while to help get her affairs in order. Family, you know. But before I do, I’m going to make sure you’re protected. This has to stay between us, do you understand?”

Douglas welled up. “Ms. Duvalle—”

“I told you to call me Ronnie.”

“Right, Ronnie. I don’t know how to thank you. You could be with your family, but you’re taking care of me. It means the world to me.”

Ronnie stood up and walked over, placing a hand on Doug’s shoulder.

“Douglas, you’re my family too,” she said, mustering up the most genuine smile she could. It clearly worked, as he hugged her.

“Thank you so much.”

“Don’t thank me yet. We have a lot of work to do to make sure you’re still around. When the smoke clears, we’ll both be on the other side, sipping strawberry mimosas.”

“Yasss!” Doug shouted in excitement.

"There is something I need you to do first."

"Anything," Doug responded.

Ronnie looked at the newspaper. She walked over and picked it out of the trash.

"Ms. Duvalle?" Doug chimed in, still waiting on her request.

"The new Burrows Industries spot for TV, where are we with that?"

"Well, Mrs. Myers signed off on everything before she left, and all the raw footage is in. We should have it done in the next few hours."

"Right. I want to look at some of the footage. I want to make some revisions using our staff, and I need it done ASAP. Tell the AV team that they're working late tonight. This has to be approved before I leave town."

"Yes, ma'am"

Ronnie walked over to Doug and affectionately squeezed his hand. "Thank you for being concerned about me. It won't go unnoticed. And don't worry about your job. I got you."

"I know you do, Ms.—I mean, Ronnie. Thank you again."

"Don't mention it again. Now get to work. There's a lot to be done in a short amount of time."

"I'm on it."

Ronnie sat back down at her desk, energized, just as she received a text message from Milton.

I'm sorry.

Under normal circumstances, she wouldn't have responded. Milton wasn't in control of anything, and it was clear that he'd been trying to inform Ronnie of that for some time now. Despite all the press to the contrary, Martin Burrows was still very much in control of Burrows Industries, and that was a problem for Ronnie and her agenda.

Milton's message was immaterial, as far as she was concerned. But there was one thing he could do.

If you really feel that way, then I'd like to take Doug off the layoff list. If I'm not getting a promotion, I can at least have my assistant back.

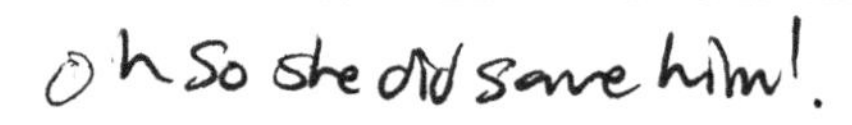

Milton replied promptly. *Done.*

Ronnie got up from her desk and walked over to the wastebasket, glancing at the newspaper. She picked it up and walked back to her desk, placing it in the center.

She looked at the paper and smirked. "Oh, this is not over. Not by a long shot."

8
POWER PLAYS

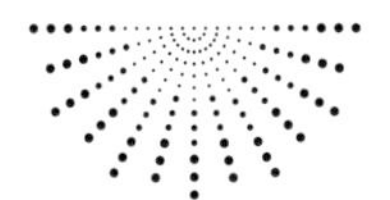

"My name is Amanda Gomez and you're watching *The Firing Line,* the number one investigative business talk show.

"Burrows Industries, a corporate darling, is now shrouded in controversy. Their latest TV ad, aimed at the average American, has left us wondering if Burrows knows what, or who, exactly that is. With me today I have Ronnie Duvalle, Vice President of Marketing at Burrows Industries, and the only person I could get on the phone to address the backlash surrounding their latest commercial."

"Thank you, Amanda, I'm glad to be—"

"Before we begin, let's look at the clip."

From her home, Ronnie watched silently as the commercial ran. In the forty-eight hours since her conversation with Martin, she had feverishly revamped the commercial, and gotten it on the most aggressive economic news show on air, with whom she was now on a live phone call.

Being on *The Firing Line* was akin to death for any firm, and now Burrows Industries was in the spotlight.

Every single person in the commercial was a middle-aged white man. In Nichelle's original casting of the commercial, there were absolutely no white men, but since she wasn't around to defend her work, it was time to throw the dagger at Martin and Nichelle. She delighted at the thought of Nichelle seeing her handiwork.

I hope that gutter ball bitch is watching right now. Serves her right for leaving with no kind of notice.

Ronnie thought of all the minorities that were replaced in each shot of the commercial as the men on-screen turned around and said the tag line: "I'm an American at Burrows Industries."

It was only a matter of time before her phone rang. She knew Milton wouldn't be able to handle the pressure.

If they only knew how inclusive this commercial was beforehand. Impressive work, gutter ball.

The plan was working extraordinarily well. She cleared her throat, not going undetected by Amanda Gomez, who was notorious for pouncing on any perceived weakness from her guest. She was just as driven as Ronnie in taking it to the next level, which is why she jumped at the opportunity to have a high-ranking executive on her show with very little notice.

As the commercial ended, Amanda went on the offensive, as predicted, using Ronnie's body language against her. "We're back. Ms. Duvalle, while the tape was rolling, it felt like you had something to say. Was it disapproval of this commercial?"

"You're right, Amanda. I was actually shaking my head in dismay at how wrong everyone is about Burrows Industries, and this commercial is misleading."

"Then why was it approved?"

"Let's be clear, I'm not defending this commercial. While it comes off a bit tone deaf, believe me when I tell you, what you just saw isn't in any way indicative of our core values, and I think anyone who has worked there would feel the same way."

"Well, not everyone, Ms. Duvalle. We've tried several times to get your president, Milton Burrows, to sit with us or even call in, and he wasn't available."

That was intentional.

Milton did not like to be blindsided, especially with something so inflammatory as this.

"Mr. Burrows is a very busy man, but I'm sure he—"

"I hate to cut you off, but this is *The Firing Line,* and I have to be frank: how tone deaf can a corporation of your magnitude be in this climate, that someone would think it was a good idea to have a commercial full of white men, and to add a red, white, and blue cherry on top, a white woman, barefoot and pregnant, in the kitchen baking a pie, saying, and I quote, 'In this business, like our country, we have no place for hyphenated Americans'?"

"Well…"

Ronnie was dying with laughter inside. The awkward silence spoke volumes in the court of public opinion. Each second she paused was a condemnation of the company and, as a result, their leadership.

She took a breath and still said nothing.

"Ms. Duvalle. we're waiting for an answer."

"Well, that's just inaccurate, Amanda," she said after what felt like an eternity to all who were watching.

"Again, if you look at our firm from my level and below, you'll see lots of diversity. In fact, we're one of the most diverse companies, not only in Houston, but in all the United States. If you look at the sta—"

"And what about the levels above yours?"

"Excuse me?" Ronnie said, pretending to be surprised by the breadcrumb.

She left Amanda to pick it up. "You said there were minorities in the firm at your level and below, of which I have no doubt."

"That's correct."

"What I'm asking you now is, how many minorities are making the real decisions for your firm? Are there any above your title? How thick is your glass ceiling?"

Checkmate.

Ronnie sat quietly, allowing her silence to condemn her employers.

For all intents and purposes, it was a disastrous interview, one surely to have not only financial implications, but ones that would put the company in reaction mode. For her, however, it was a dream come true.

Her final breadcrumb was nibbled up by Amanda's aggressiveness, and she'd played right into Ronnie's hands.

If the board wouldn't promote her, she'd turn a spotlight on their practices.

In less than ten minutes, she'd tanked their stock price, given Martin a potential heart attack, reignited the discussion for her position as Senior Vice President and, above all else, made herself untouchable from being fired. Any retaliatory action against her now would cause massive lawsuits, workforce commission investigations and more press. She'd be lauded as a whistleblower, an empathic victim of another heartless corporation's ambition.

All she had to do now was stick the landing. "I…I can't comment on internal affairs at the firm. What I can tell you, Amanda, is that Burrows Industries is one of the best places to work in the country."

"As long as you're a white man."

"I didn't say that."

"You didn't have to. The commercial says it all."

"Amanda, I just don't think you're giving the firm a fair shake."

"Well, I see we won't get much more from you, or anyone else at your firm, so I want to end this interview and thank you, Ms. Duvalle, for coming on *The Firing Line*."

The segment ended, but Ronnie stayed on the line. After a few moments, Amanda said. "Ms. Duvalle, I want to let you know it wasn't personal. It's my job to ask the hard-hitting questions, and I take my job seriously."

"I can appreciate that, Amanda. It was rough, but we all have a job to do."

"If you don't mind me asking, off the record, you seem to be a very sharp woman. What really happened with this commercial?"

"This stays off the record?"

"Of course."

"It caught me by surprise, too. The commercial no doubt speaks for itself. I don't think there's any coincidence that the face sent to fix this fiasco had to look like mine. I'm taking bereavement time for my brother-in-law's funeral, so it was a lot to take in."

"And I just put you in the firing line...I feel terrible. Listen, Ronnie, if it's okay with you, I'll make sure to mention how much duress you were under. I think it's important for our viewers to know what an actual leader looks like while the CEO is hiding out."

"You don't have to do that, Amanda. It's my job to fall on the sword for the company."

"You do your job, and I'll do mine. There's no way I'm letting another woman look bad if I can help it."

"Thank you, Amanda. I really appreciate you."

"My pleasure, Ronnie. I'm sorry for your loss."

"Thank you."

She hung up the phone. Already a clip of the show was going viral. Martin would receive her message anytime now.

well everyone is going to know she authorized the changes. They can fire her

9
LOYALTY AND BETRAYAL

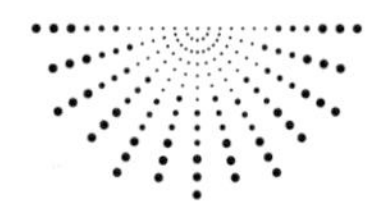

'Now entering Breaux Bridge', the sign read as she sped down the highway.

"This fucking place," she muttered to herself.

Breaux Bridge was home, but it was a small corner of hell she'd never wanted to return to. For the past three hours, she'd been listening to Lucas' playlists she'd downloaded.

"Honestly, all I ever really liked was a few 90s R&B songs and trap music until I met your father." she said to the companion in her womb.

Typically, she hated road trips, but there was a lot to think about on this trip. Being told there wouldn't be a minority senior vice president, and Kendra coming back, were problems, but Lucas lying in a coma was a much larger concern, trumped by the question of if she should keep his baby or not.

She hadn't really spent a lot of time or energy on the matter. She'd been firmly against having a child out of wedlock, and she'd never planned on getting married, but falling in love hadn't been on the agenda either.

Lucas complicated things. His request and his subsequent coma were an anchor of shit luck she wanted to remove. Martin had thrown a wrench in her plans, and Kendra coming back to Houston was only going to make things more difficult, so she needed time to regroup.

She hated leaving Lucas, but Walter and Natalie had both been supportive when she'd gone by the hospital to tell them she was leaving. The couple assured her to take as much time as she needed. She'd grown to care deeply for the Kimbles over the past few weeks. Ronnie wondered if Walter had told Natalie about the pregnancy.

They are married after all. There should be no secrets between a husband and wife.

"Of course, he didn't. Walter is a man of his word." She mumbled aloud.

Entering the city limits, derision flooded through her. "Home," she scoffed.

Her phone chimed, and she connected it to the Bluetooth. She'd been expecting the call.

"This is Ronnie."

"You fucking bitch!"

"I'm sorry, who is this?"

"You know goddamn well who this is, Ronnie. You snake ass mother—"

"Nichelle? So, I take it, you've seen the commercial?"

"You mean *my* commercial? What did you do to it?"

"This wasn't personal, Nichelle. I was—"

"Personal? Bitch, we are way past that. You've got some motherfucking nerve! How dare you rebrand *my* commercial? I know hard work doesn't mean a damn thing to a hoe like you, where every promotion comes with a Plan B pill, but my name is everything to me, Ronnie. It's my name all over that damn project!"

"Is there a point to your melodrama today, or do you just want to bitch for bitching's sake?"

"You took my man, that's cool. I was foul to him, so you got him. You lay off all those employees, fine. Let karma deal with your ass. But you sully my name? My fucking name? Bitch, you must be on that dope. I will drag your ass—"

"Let me cut you off right there, Ms. Sweet Valley High. I don't know if you think you're—"

"No, bitch, let me cut *you* off right there. If you think you can ruin my name, you don't know me very well. You must've forgotten who gave you that black eye. I will fuck you up. Do not play with me, Ronnie!"

She'd seen Nichelle upset before, but not like this. She was slurring her words. She already knew the answer, but asked the question anyway. "Are you drunk, Nichelle? Or are you deep into your Tupac playlist?"

"It's none of your damn business what I am. All you need to know is, if you keep playing with me, you will get hurt. Trust."

"So that's what's happening? You must be on administrative leave to detox. Didn't realize the company gave leaves of absence for binge-drinking and hurt feelings."

"Motherfuck you, Ronnie. People like you can only get away with your bullshit for so long. Eventually the world will see through your façade, and you'll get everything you deserve, and when the day comes – when karma finally catches up with all the plotting and backstabbing you've done for the sake of your ego – I hope I'm sitting front and center to witness your fall."

"Us."

"Excuse me?"

"People like us, Nichelle."

"Bitch, I'm *nothing* like you."

Ronnie chuckled. "It's truly fascinating that you believe that. Here I am, the self-serving bitch that angers you to the point of a drunk-dial because of a terrible commercial that needed tons of work, and—"

"Bitch, you know that commercial was good. You're just jealous—"

"—and yet," she continued, "if you were actually doing your job – you know at work – instead of day-drinking, you would've been here to prevent any changes to your vision."

"That doesn't give you the right—"

"And while you chew on that, is it too early to point out that you walked out on two of the nicest people you could ever meet in their time of crisis? Oh, and not once have you asked how anyone is doing, specifically the man you claim to have loved?"

There was a pause on the phone. After a spell Nichelle said. "I…I had a lot going on that night."

"Oh, I'm sure. *Us* self-serving bitches usually do. But so did Lucas, and the Kimbles. Hell, they're still reliving that night. I still relive that night. Have you even called to check on them?"

"Well, I—"

"That was completely rhetorical, because we both know the answer. Now, if you're done making felony-level threats, I'm going to get off the phone. Make sure you take a BC powder for your inevitable hangover."

Ronnie was about to hang up the phone when Nichelle asked, "How is he?"

The question made Ronnie swerve the car. Regaining her composure, she rubbed her face with her right palm, keeping her left hand on the wheel.

After a giant sigh, she responded to the awkward question. "Let me get this straight. You just threatened to beat my ass, and you think I'm gonna tell you—"

"Damn it, Ronnie, you won. You won everything, okay? You got the man, the job, everything. Just tell me how he's doing."

Ronnie rolled her eyes. She wanted to hang up the phone, but she knew exactly how Nichelle felt. The truth of the matter was, she'd been no different than Nichelle on that night. She'd wanted to run and forget the name Lucas Kimble ever existed; wanted to find an excuse not to be at the hospital. The fear had made her show up.

She recognized herself in Nichelle's actions and truly didn't blame her one bit. In truth, there could have been a small part of her that stayed that night only because of their rivalry. A piece of her, however small, acknowledged that she may have stayed only because Nichelle had left.

"He has a subdural hematoma and he's in a medically-induced coma. They don't have any prognosis beyond that."

There was a brief silence on the phone. Ronnie was about to hang up when Nichelle asked another question. "Are the Kimbles okay?"

"Well, no. Like I said, their son is in a medically-induced coma after being shot. But they're strong people; they're dealing with it the best way they can. Natalie has read half the bible, and Walter…well, he's been there for Natalie."

"He's a good man."

"That he is," Ronnie agreed.

There was a pause in the conversation as they both aligned in their mutual admiration for the Kimble family. Ronnie thought about the wedding ring, and how Nichelle had given it to her despite their tension.

It was time to clear the air. "Look, Nichelle, the commercial thing wasn't personal. There's a lot going on at work, and—"

Whirp.

Her statement was interrupted by the sound of a police siren.

Ronnie took a deep breath. "Here we fucking go."

10
ROAD TO PERDITION

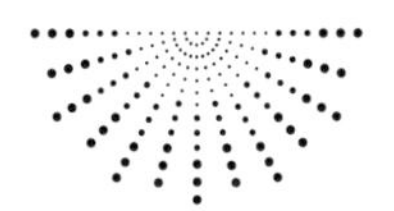

"Look, Nichelle, I'm going to have to call you back. I'm getting pulled over."

"Okay, well, I hope they lock your ass up for whatever it is."

"And we're back."

She hung up the phone, frustrated that she'd bothered to offer an olive branch, but that would have to wait.

She was on a two-lane road in the middle of nowhere and didn't have the best experience with police. It was now night with an overcast fog.

She'd grown up here, so she knew the officers, and cringed at the idea of which officer might have stopped her. She thought of grabbing her phone to record the interaction, but thought that may escalate things. Instead, she got her driver's license and insurance, and extended her arm out of the window as the officer was approaching. Her pulse quickened.

She tried to make eye contact with the officer as he shone his flashlight into her car, obscuring her vision, instantly making her regret the decision to not record.

"Good evening, ma'am. Driver's license and registration."

"Honestly, officer, I don't know why you pulled me over. I wasn't speed—"

The officer cut her off. "Ma'am! Step out of the vehicle."

Stay calm, she told herself.

It was too late to grab her phone.

She opened the door and stepped out of the vehicle, the flashlight still in her face. She wasn't sure which officer it was, but she was regretting her trip entirely.

"Okay, Officer, I'm out now. I'm going to need your badge number—"

The flashlight turned off. She looked at the cop and smiled. "Son of a bitch, Devon Flynn! Somebody made you a cop?"

The officer handed her license back as Ronnie gave one of her oldest friends a hug. She punched him playfully in his arm. "I should kick your ass for what you just did to me! Why did you pull me over in the first place?"

"Now, you know we don't get any new traffic around these parts. Once I ran your plates and saw it was you, I had to pull you over. I thought you'd never come back to this place. How have you been?"

"Besides the bullshit, life's great. What about you, *Officer* Flynn?"

"Oh, you know, busting caps in people's asses. Protect and serve, shit like that."

The pair chuckled.

"Same old goofball, huh?"

"Goofball with a gun now. I'm a double G," he replied, pretending to throw up gang signs, evoking more laughs. "I didn't think I'd ever see you again. You must be here for Rue."

"Yeah, her husband died."

"Yeah, I know. She's gonna be mighty surprised to see you. She didn't think you were comin'."

Ronnie smirked at Devon's creole accent and the fact that, after all these years, he obviously still had feelings for her sister. "So, you've talked to my sister since her husband died?"

"Well, I…I, uh, offered my condolences," Devon replied. His eyes shifted toward the ground.

Ronnie grinned devilishly. “Boy, the ground ain’t even dug yet, and you trying to get some widow pussy?”

“What? It’s not like that, Ronnie, I swear.”

“Oh, Devon Flynn. I guess it’s true that some things never change.”

As Ronnie laughed, Devon took a couple of steps closer to her as she taunted him. “Damn it, Ronnie, things do change. Do you have to be so vulgar?”

“Aw, you mad ’cause I said *pussy*? What did you want me to say, ‘coochie’?”

“That’s better.”

“Negro, we’re grown now. Besides, the one thing you haven’t denied is that you’re trying to tap that ass.”

“Oh, come on, Ronnie! This is your sister we’re talking about.”

“Devon wants some pus-say. Pus-say pus-say Pus-say. Devon trying to get my sister’s Pus-say,” she sang as she danced.

Devon, now flustered, muttered, “You keep doing this shit, I’m gonna shoot you.”

“Okay, well, your secret is safe with me, Detective Dick’em Down, though might I point out, you’ve been asking me to hook you up with her since junior high.”

“Ronnie…”

“Taste the yams.”

“Ron—”

“Dig in them guts.”

“You’re such an asshole.”

She looked at her now thoroughly-embarrassed friend and realized she had pushed far enough. “Okay, Officer, you have the right to remain silent...for now.” She smiled at her friend, who sighed in relief of the conversation ending.

“So how far is your wet dream’s – I mean, my sister’s house from here?”

“I remember now why I was glad you left.”

“Her house, Dick’em Down?”

“Okay, chill – and that’s not gonna become a thing. You know, the old Anderson plantation? Rue and her husband bought that a few years back."

"Damn, that's a big house."

"Yeah, she's got a butler and everything. I'm getting off in a few hours, I can come by after—"

"I want to kick it with you, Dev, but I'm tired. All I want to do is talk with my sister for an hour and then sleep."

"Well, I'm not getting in the middle of that, but we're gonna hang before you leave town, okay?"

"You got it, detective."

"I'm an officer."

"No, you're a detective…of the Dick'em down variety," she cackled.

"That is not gonna become a thing, Ronnie."

"It already is. Devon Flynn is Detective Dick'em Down, AKA Triple D!"

"I can't believe this shit. You're not even in town five seconds and you're bullying me, a grown man with a gun. This ain't high school."

"I could just go back to calling you Tink Tink."

"Damn it! I peed in the bed one time! I was six!"

"One time is one time too many, Triple D. And you wonder why you can't get in my sister's pants."

"I keep warning you, don't make me fill out this paperwork. I'll make you a hashtag real quick."

Ronnie hugged her friend again. "It was good to see you, Dev. Let me go and see what this heifer is up to."

She got in the car.

Before she left, she hit the horn and yelled out, "Bye, Triple D!"

She rolled up her window, driving off, still chuckling about the entire thing.

Seeing Devon cut her apprehension about coming to Breaux Bridge in half.

Maybe this won't be half bad.

11
SISTERS

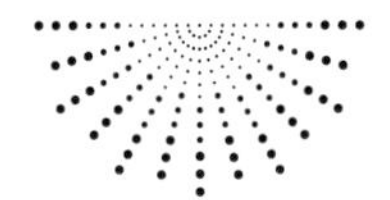

"Well, we're here. I don't know how long we're here for, but we're here."

She parked her car in the driveway of her sister's home.

She couldn't get over how well Rue had done for herself. Though her married name was Guillaume, she was still a Duvalle and, if nothing else, she knew how to survive. From the looks of her home, she'd done just that and then some.

Ivory columns supported a full-length balcony sitting above the twelve-foot doors at the entrance. The garden looked to have been manicured that day. The gravel in the driveway seemed new. There was a deliberate southern charm to it all; it fit Rue perfectly.

She hesitated to get out of the car. It had been forever since she'd seen her sister. She had left everyone and everything here behind.

The enormity of what she was about to do settled in her. The doubt and regret crept in.

"I can't do this," she said aloud.

The trip was a waste, and she wouldn't prolong it anymore.

She had put the car in reverse and backed out of the driveway when she heard a horn.

A white Range Rover with a hard black top blocked her exit.

A five-foot-five slender woman with dark caramel skin stepped out of the car, wearing a fitted black T-shirt and gray spandex pants. Her ginger-brown hair was straightened and in a ponytail.

Ronnie closed her eyes.

Fuck, shit, fuck.

She parked the car and rolled down the window to greet her big sister.

"*Ma chère*? Is that you, Ronnie?"

"It's me," Ronnie said, smiling reluctantly.

"You made it. I'm…"

"Impressed?"

"Surprised, for sure. I guess you could say impressed as well."

Ronnie got out of the car and stood silently. There was a long pause before Rue finally asked, "Well, how have you been?"

"I'm fine, Rue. I was—"

"You were just deciding that you were going to turn around and leave. I know. I've been where you are. But you're here now, and it's a long drive back to Houston, so you might as well rest a while. Ain't no sense getting back on the road just yet. Besides, what's the use of driving three hours, just to get here and turn around, without having some crawfish etouffee?"

The idea of eating sounded good. Still, she didn't like the idea of her sister presuming anything about her. "I wasn't leaving, Rue. I was just making sure this was the right house."

"Of course, you were. My mistake. In either case, you're here."

"You know what? This was a mistake. I'm—"

"Ronnie, you don't have to be defensive. Like it or not, you're home, and I need you here – if not for me, then for Malcolm. Now, are you going to come over here and give me a hug?"

Ronnie rolled her eyes and embraced her sister, who held on to her much longer than she was comfortable with. But the longer the hug continued, the more comfortable she became. There was odd calmness towards it – the kind of hug that only family can give. It was the first time she'd felt relaxed since Lucas had been shot. With all the drama in her life, a hug was exactly what she needed.

She pulled her sister closer, tears flowing from her eyes.

"Shhh, it's okay. I've prayed for this day. Lord knows, I've prayed for this day," Rue said as she clasped her.

Ronnie wiped her eyes. "Okay, enough of that."

"Well, that was short-lived, but fun. Why don't we go inside? Bradley will get your bags."

Rue beckoned a tall, strapping, light-skinned man who came out to help.

"Bradley? So, you have a butler now?"

"I do. He's been kind enough to help while we get through this difficult transition."

Ronnie looked the butler over once more. He was certainly attractive – too attractive to be a butler, in her opinion. "Is that all he's helping with?"

"I know it's been a while since we've been around each other, so I won't respond to that, because you're tired. Bradley is a very loyal member of this family."

"Okay. None of my business."

Rue walked into the kitchen and then came out flustered.

"I'm sorry, I forgot Cynthia has the night off. We're on our own. I haven't gone shopping, but I can make you something."

"I'm fine, really."

"I keep Cookie Crisp in the pantry, because I know how much you like it."

"Don't presume to know me, Rue. I don't even eat cereal anymore, especially Cookie Crisp. I just want to find a bed to lay down and get this over with."

"I'll pour you a bowl." Rue ignored her entirely.

Ronnie walked into the kitchen and sat at the island while her sister poured almond milk into the cereal.

She took a bite and said, "I'm only eating this to not be rude."

"Thank you, you're so considerate," Rue retorted.

Ronnie continued to eat the cereal. By her third bite, her sister was smirking.

"A joke you mind sharing with the class?" Ronnie asked.

"Nothing. Nothing at all."

"Oh, no. That's the famous Rue goody-two-shoes smirk. It absolutely means something."

Rue poured herself a bowl and sat in front of her sister. "It's just, I'm sure the people you work with would lose their minds if they saw you sitting here, eating a bowl of Cookie Crisp like a ten-year-old."

Ronnie poured more cereal into the bowl. "Well, I can't say you're wrong. I don't even know why I like it. I didn't expect you to remember."

"*Chile,* please. All you ever talked about every morning was Cookie Crisp. We could have pancakes, bacon, and eggs, or a whole Cajun spread, and you'd want your Cookie Crisp!"

Ronnie looked down at the bowl. "I mean, it's good cereal."

The two laughed. After a pause, Rue looked at her sister again. "She asked if you were coming."

"She wasted her breath."

"Ronnie, she just wants to know if you're okay."

"Good, you can tell her I am."

"Momma said—"

"Don't." Ronnie pointed at her sister with the spoon, the mood becoming very tense.

Ronnie stood up as Rue said, "She's sick, Ronnie. She wants to see you before the funeral."

"Damn it, Rue!"

"What?"

"I did not drive three hours to reopen old wounds. I came to pay my respects. You can tell Van that I'm fine, and if she has questions, she can keep them to herself."

Ronnie walked off but quickly turned around. "I just came back for the cereal." She grabbed the bowl and then stormed away.

Rue followed her, determined not to give up. "She's in rehab, Ronnie."

The statement worked.

Ronnie stopped in her tracks. She didn't turn around, but she stood motionless as Rue continued.

"She's been there for months now. She hasn't left, she hasn't fallen off the wagon; she's there and she's getting better. Even put on some weight. I know that's a lot to take in. She didn't have a sober week when we were growing up."

"Hell, she didn't have a sober *day*."

"She's had months of sobriety now. She's not who you remember."

Ronnie chewed the cereal, which was getting soggy at his point. "Rue, I've worked damn hard to put our past behind me."

"There's no pressure, but before you decide, you should know that I invited her to stay with me, and she said she wanted to give you space, should you come. Just hear her out. If I can forgive her, maybe you can, too."

"I'll give her ten minutes."

"That's a start."

Ronnie handed the bowl to her sister and went to her room. As she got ready for the night, her phone buzzed. A message from Milton Burrows.

What the hell have you done?

12
BLOOD TIES

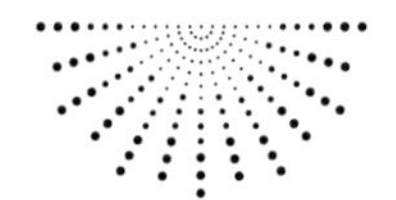

I can't believe I let this heifer talk me into this.

Ahead of Ronnie and Rue was the Breaux Bridge Rehabilitation and Recovery Center.

The building itself hadn't been updated since the late 80s, the grass in the front unkempt, weeds surfacing through the sidewalk. The stair rails leading to the building had a considerable amount of rust on them, and the white letters on the welcome sign were mildewed.

Ronnie walked to the front door and walked in.

The interior mirrored its outside appearance. The facility reeked of lime and old cafeteria food. She'd been spending so much time in hospitals lately, the scent was familiar yet nauseating.

The intense desire to leave overtook her, when her sister rubbed her back.

"You've come this far, Ronnie. Please, life is too short. You don't want things to go unsaid."

"If she starts up, you probably aren't gonna like what I have to say."

"I don't have to. This isn't for me, it's for you – the both of you."

Her sister was right; she had a lot to say, and there would probably never be another time to say it.

After passing through reception to the patient lounge, Ronnie spotted Vanessa Clayton sitting in a rocking chair, watching Jerry Springer on TV.

A rush of emotion overwhelmed her. Ronnie hadn't seen her, called her, or answered her calls since she'd left Breaux Bridge.

The overwhelming urge to throw up took over, and she rushed to the nearest trash can.

Rue handed Ronnie one of the towels in the room. As she cleaned her face, she glanced at Vanessa. She looked more frail than she'd remembered.

There were words to be said, but she wouldn't break the ice.

Thankfully, Rue was there to interject. "Momma, look who's here to see you."

"Did that check come in yet, Rue?"

"Not yet, momma."

What check? Ronnie thought to herself.

Vanessa looked over briefly and then back at the TV. Clearly Ronnie would have to break the silence between them. She rolled her eyes and looked at Rue, who nudged her forward.

"Hey, Van," Ronnie finally muttered.

The woman looked over at Ronnie again, finally diverting her attention from the TV. "How far along are you?"

"Van, what are you—"

"You're getting fat, and I don't think I've ever seen you throw up, so how far along are you?" she replied.

"Momma, what are you talking about? Ronnie's skinny as a twig, she's not—"

"I am pregnant, Rue."

As Rue looked at her in disbelief, Vanessa said, "Damn, girl, how did you let that happen to you?"

"See, Van, when two people care about each other—"

"Don't play with me, little girl. Who did you con into making this baby with you?"

"I didn't con anyone. His name is Lucas Kimble." Ronnie said, abandoning the urge to defend herself.

Vanessa looked confused. "That name sounds familiar. Is he from around here?"

"No."

"I could've sworn I'd heard that name before."

"He's not from here. You don't know him. Now can we please move on?"

"Ronnie's right, Momma, let's just move on."

Van took a cigarette from her pack of Marlboro 100s and pulled a drag. "Well, enjoy it while it lasts."

"What's that supposed to mean?"

"It means, he doesn't know you. Not the real you, but he will."

Arms folded, Ronnie shook her head. "He does, actually. He sees the real me. I'm not afraid to show him because he's not afraid to see it." Vanessa put out her cigarette and lit another and after a few puffs said.

"The thing about scorpions is, no matter how much they try to change their nature, they sting, because they're motherfucking scorpions. That's what you are, Ronnie. If you haven't stung him already, you will, and when you do, he's going to see what he's really gotten himself into."

"Well, we can't all be as lucky as Vanessa, to have such a prominent husband like the Reverend Reginald Clayton Jr. Speaking of which, I wonder what – or who – he's been getting himself into?"

"Kimble! That's the boy from the news. The one that got shot by a cop, ain't it?" Vanessa interjected.

Ronnie rolled her eyes, looking at Rue. "You know what? I tried."

"Ronnie, please."

"No, Rue, she's intolerable. I'll catch a share ride back to your place, if you're staying here to deal with this mess of a woman. Goodbye, Van."

Ronnie stormed out of the building and called for a car.

It wasn't long before Rue stormed out of the building behind her. "Ronnie, wait. I'm sorry, but you know Momma, she—"

"For the love of God, Van is not our mom! I don't know why you insist on calling her that. Sometimes I wonder if you even remember our actual mother."

"Of course, I remember her."

"Well, each time you call that... thing in there 'Momma', it spits on the memory of your actual mother. Victoria Duvalle. *She,*" Ronnie pointed to the building behind them, "was no one's mother. Hell, she wasn't even a decent aunt."

"Ronnie, you've got to learn grace."

"Don't tell me what to learn. I didn't come here for a lecture. I came to pay my respects, because you said you needed me to be here, but this was a mistake."

Her car pulled up. She opened the door and got in without saying another word to her sister.

When she arrived at the house, she went to pack her things.

"I don't know why I even came here," she muttered to herself.

She was descending the stairs with her suitcase when the front door opened.

"Yo, Ronnie!" Devon said as he walked in, blocking her exit. "Hey! What's wrong?"

"Move, Triple D. I'm getting out of this hellscape. That woman has some damn nerve."

"Ronnie, take a breath. Which woman?"

Before she could respond, she became queasy again, and scrambled out the door to the grass, suffering another bout of morning sickness.

"Damn it!" she yelled in frustration as Devon slowly approached her.

"Ronnie, are you o—"

"I'm fine. I just need some water and fresh air."

As she sat on the grass, Devon sat on the ground next to her. "I guess you went to see Van."

"She's a habitual line crosser. After all these years, that woman still knows how to push my buttons. I don't even know how she and Rue are even on speaking terms now. They hated each other."

"Maybe because she got tired of feeling angry. You haven't been here a while, but you remember how wild Rue was. She was hurt and angry, and when she found Malcolm, she stayed away for a good while. It wasn't until he got sick that Rue really started coming around again. "

"Sounds like you've been keeping tabs on my sister."

Devon threw his hands in the air. "Alright, fine. I'm sweet on your sister. You happy?"

Ronnie chuckled. "I'm just happy that you're being honest with yourself."

"I know you've always known. She's just always done it for me."

"There were so many times I wanted to tell her."

That gave Devon pause. "Why didn't you?"

"You're my boy, Dev. Besides, it would be better coming from you."

"Yeah. It just never seemed like the right time."

"So, tell her now."

"Ronnie, her husband just died."

"And? He's not gonna be more dead tomorrow. If I've learned anything over the past few weeks, it's that love is a wonderful feeling. When it's gone, all you think about is when you'll be able to have it again. Life is short, Dev. Say the things you need to say to the people you care about."

Devon nodded and looked at his friend. "Sounds like some good advice you should take yourself."

"Dev, don't even start—"

"There's a reason you came home. Now, I'm not sure if it is to talk to Rue, or to Van, but as hopeful as Malcolm was in you returning, I think he knew in the back of his mind you weren't ever gonna look back."

Ronnie thought about his words. He made a solid point; she could've just showed up to the funeral and left right after. "I'm pregnant."

He looked flabbergasted. "You're what?"

"Why is everyone surprised by this?"

"I'm not surprised, I'm... okay, I'm a little surprised, but that's because you've never said one thing about having a family."

"I know. It sounds crazy when I say it out loud. The thing is, the more I say it, the more I'm coming around to the idea. Until I saw Van."

Devon sat next to his friend and said, "Van's gonna be Van. Nothing you can do about that. Don't let her get in your head." Ronnie nodded in agreement as Devon asked,

"So, who's the lucky guy?"

She smirked and shook her head. "Have you been watching the news?"

"When I can."

"You heard about the guy in Houston who was shot by the police?"

"Yeah.... Wait, don't tell me he's the father?"

"He was going to propose the night he got shot."

"Damn, Ronnie. I didn't know."

"How could you? Look, none of that matters now. The important takeaway is: you need to talk to Rue."

Devon nodded in agreement. "Tell you what. I'll talk to Rue if you clear the air with Van."

"Now, you know I—"

"I know you need to do this for yourself, and for that little bun in the oven. It's time to heal, Ronnie."

She leaned on his shoulder and nodded. "You know, when I left here, I wasn't leaving you."

"I know. I'm just glad you're back, however long we have you."

She kissed him on his cheek, which he promptly wiped off. "Ugh, nobody wants your throw-up kisses. Go brush your teeth," he joked.

The pair chuckled.

"I've missed you, Triple D."

"I told you, that will not become a thing."

"Whatever you say, Detective."

Devon stood up and helped Ronnie to her feet, and the two exchanged a hug. Devon picked up her suitcase and was about to go inside when he stopped. "Something else you should know, because I don't want you to be blindsided."

"What?"

"Rue's letting Pastor Clayton do the funeral."

"What in the holy hell?"

"Like I said, Rue has turned a corner in forgiveness. I even heard that she's donating a large sum of money to the church. Please don't leave. I just wanted you to be prepared."

Ronnie took a long pause and looked at her surroundings. Her sister needed her in more ways than one. She grabbed her suitcase from Devon. "Don't worry, I'm not going anywhere."

13
THE PASTOR

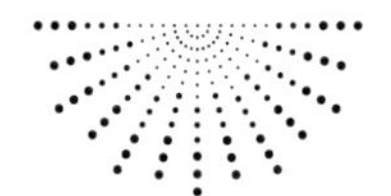

The stock price is still tanking.

Ronnie went online to watch the fallout of her interview continue to pick up steam.

She put her phone away and looked at her sister, who was still reading the bible.

Lord, I sure could use an edible right now. She thought.

As they sat in the car, she wondered why they didn't have the funeral at the church. She hadn't been there in years. Still, she found it odd that the pastor had agreed to do the entire funeral outside. Since Devon had told her about Rue giving money to the church, her mind had been in overdrive.

This girl can't be that stupid.

When they were younger, the pastor had been a pillar in the community, and the assistant police chief renowned for taking in two little girls who'd lost their mother. Yet he also was a drunk and a gambling degenerate who'd made their lives a living nightmare.

He and Rue were like oil and water.

Ronnie wanted answers, but knew now wasn't the time. Still, she knew there had to be more to the story.

When this is over, I'll call Doug and have him look into the pastor's finances.

"Don't worry, Momma isn't buried here," Rue interrupted her thoughts.

She didn't want to admit it, but there was a sense of relief that they weren't going there. She didn't want to process that just yet – if at all.

Her sister continued reading her bible. Ronnie wanted to be there for her but didn't know how. Comfort was not in their family's nature.

As the limo pulled up, Ronnie asked, "What verse are you reading?"

"Lamentations 2:17."

Ronnie smirked. "'The Lord has done what He purposed; He has fulfilled His word, Which He commanded in days of old.'"

"I see someone still remembers bible study."

"How could I forget? One thing about the pastor: he knows how to beat the Bible into children. I'm assuming Reggie is doing the service."

Rue's eyes widened, confirming what Devon had told her. Ronnie persisted. "Why didn't you tell me?"

"Devon told you, didn't he?"

"This isn't about him, and you know it."

"Honestly, I wanted you to be here and, considering how well your chat with Momma went, it wasn't a topic I thought you'd be up to discussing."

"Why aren't you having a funeral in the church?"

"Malcolm didn't want a big fuss. Besides, I thought you'd prefer it this way."

"You didn't do this for me. Who does he owe?"

"The church has been under renovation. It was just easier this way."

Ronnie nodded. "I see. And just how is the church paying for these renovations?"

"I'm not following."

"What I mean is, how much of these renovations is coming from the congregation, and how much is coming out of your pocket?"

"Ronnie, now's not the time."

"It's definitely the time. I don't understand, after everything that man put us through, how you would—"

"I am burying my husband today!" Rue yelled in a moment of vulnerability. A few tears rolled from her eyes, and Ronnie handed her a tissue. After a spell Rue said, "We can talk about this later. Now is not the time."

"We'll table it, for now."

Ronnie got out of the car with her sister as they arrived at the grave site. She accompanied Rue to the front row next to the mausoleum, sitting in the front row, when she saw him.

Pastor Reginald Clayton Jr. Better known as Pastor Reggie.

Ronnie looked at the clean-shaven, brown-skinned man. She remembered him as a physically-intimidating force. His bald head gleamed in the sunlight. He saw her and opened his arms wide. "Weeping may endure a night but joy cometh in the morning."

The pastor leaned in to hug Ronnie, who stopped him with a raised hand. "That's far enough."

She took her seat, almost nauseous at the scent of his Nautica cologne. The pastor smiled as he looked to his congregation. "That's my youngest, y'all. I guess some things never change."

There was an awkward chuckle from the congregation.

Ronnie watched as the man who'd raised her began his service.

"Brother Malcolm Guillaume was a good man," the pastor began.

Ronnie discreetly put in her earbuds to block out the sound of his voice. From what she could tell, the service was short but powerful. As much as she didn't like him, Ronnie had to admit Reggie knew how to work an audience. The moment he opened his mouth, otherwise intelligent people became followers, feeding his ego.

It truly angered her that her sister was among them.

Almost on cue, Ronnie felt her sister's pinch. "I don't ask you for anything, but please take those dang things out of your ears and show some respect, if for no one other than Malcolm," she whispered furiously.

Ronnie nodded and removed the headphones. As she did, her eyes connected with the pastor's. He was finishing up his sermon and liked to bring people up to the stage.

Ronnie shook her head dismissively at him. He smiled and continued his sermon.

Recognizing the moment, Rue leaned in. "Ronnie—"

"I'm not doing it, Rue."

"I know—"

"I don't live in his house, and I don't owe him a damn thing. Neither do you."

Rue leaned back and nodded, letting go of the tense moment. After a spell, she leaned back in. "Ronnie, I know what you're thinking. If he calls you up, just say something nice and sit back down."

Ronnie shook her head dismissively but Rue leaned in again. "This is my husband's funeral. Let him have peace, please."

"What happens next is up to him. If he calls me up there, I make no promises."

Rue leaned back.

Ronnie knew Reggie well enough that he'd call her unspoken bluff – except she wasn't bluffing.

As the sermon ended and they laid the body into the ground, Pastor Reggie said, "We have a special visitor all the way from Houston, Texas. Now, as y'all know, this young lady was like a daughter to me. In fact, even though she's not my blood, I treat her as one of my own. Y'all may know her as Veronica, but I call her Ronnie. Come on up, and say something to the people."

Ronnie looked at her sister and smirked.

Rue grabbed her to prevent her from getting up. "Ronnie, please."

"You heard what the pastor said. Can't keep the good people of Mount Ebenezer Baptist waiting."

She smirked as she walked to the microphone, taking it from the pastor. "Thank you, Pastor Reggie. Good old pastor and his church. Malcolm Guillaume was the most decent man I'd ever met, and when I found out he'd gone to the other side, for a moment I wasn't going to come home. In fact, I never thought I'd set foot in this town again, but here I am standing in front of a bunch of familiar faces and what it has helped remind me of is, there's nothing like family. Can I get an amen?"

She was silent as the crowd clapped. The pastor was about to walk over when Ronnie took the mike from the stand and walked between the aisles among the people. "I respected Malcolm. He was a credit to Breaux Bridge, Louisiana, and a decent man.

"Amen," shouted a member of the congregation.

"And so, I came to pay my respects to a good, decent man."

"Take your time, sister." Another member of the congregation said.

"It would be years before I met another of Malcolm's caliber. This year, in fact. So, in all of my life, I only met two decent men. Oh, I can't forget about Pastor Reggie."

The crowd clapped as they heard the Pastor's name.

Ronnie continued. "Pastor Reggie, the kind of man who convinced his wife that she needed sleeping meds, then anxiety meds, then mood elevators, then mood stabilizers, all so he could get his dick wet without a divorce. No, I didn't forget about Pastor Reggie. There's not a decent bone in his body."

The congregation murmured as Reggie walked up to her, attempting to pull the microphone from her hands.

Ronnie pushed him away. "Get you damn hands off me!"

"I won't have any more disrespect in the Lord's house." He reached for the microphone again and Ronnie slapped him.

The congregation gasped in shock.

The pastor held his face for a moment, nodding, as he gently took the microphone from Ronnie. He turned to his congregation, then back to Ronnie. "This is a time of healing. Now, Ronnie, let me say that, as your surrogate father and pastor, I forgive you. The emotions of today have to be hard to handle, and it's natural to lash out, so I'll take the blame. But as an officer of the law, I can't allow you to slap a police officer in broad daylight. You're under arrest."

Lol

14
LIVING ON THE EDGE

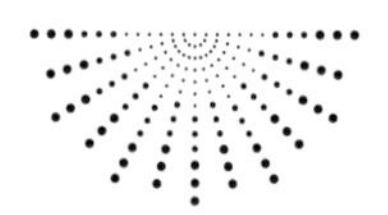

Ronnie sat in the back of the police car in silence. She tried to calm herself, but she didn't care about the consequences of her actions. She was more worried about Rue and how upset she had to be.

"I see you're still a little hellspawn."

"Learned from the best, Reggie."

He shook his head and turned off the main road, away from the police station. After roughly a quarter mile, he stopped the car on the side of the road.

Ronnie looked out the window to the marshy swamp land as Reggie asked, "When are you leaving town?"

"Well, I was leaving right after the funeral, but now I'm thinking I'll stay and take in some of the scenery. Maybe slap a few more pastors."

Reggie chuckled chillingly. "You know, not that long ago, they found out a gator ate Ms. Alberta's niece? She was from out of town and not used to the way things work around here – thought she could make her own rules. One day she went fishing over by the Phillips' pond. Gator snatched her right up. All they found was her arm. Just goes to show you, no matter how quiet a place is, there's danger everywhere."

"Lucky for me, a crowd of eyewitnesses saw me leave the gravesite with you, so getting eaten by an alligator would be hard to explain, wouldn't you say?"

Reggie laughed. "Hard, but not impossible."

"You're welcome to take your best shot, Reg, but I'm not sure it's going to work out the way it did when I was five."

"Is that what this is about? Listen, your mother's death was ruled a suici—"

"You can save that horse shit for Rue, or Van, or anyone else that wasn't there."

There was a pregnant pause in the car before Reggie broke it. "You know, since the day you were born, you've been nothing but trouble."

"Fuck you, Reggie. Take me to jail or—"

"You better remember who you're talking to, Ronnie. I'll put my foot in your ass and have you shitting shoe polish."

"There he is! That's the Reggie I know. Remember the last time you tried that, Pastor? You thought I'd go running to your little flunky, Chief Stevens, but I knew you had everyone brainwashed in this damn town, so I called Child Protective Services."

Reggie nodded. "I'll admit, that was cute, but you ain't no kid anymore. Ain't no one coming to help you."

"You're absolutely right. I'm not a kid anymore, and I don't need help. So the real question you should be asking yourself is: if you didn't stand a chance against me then, what makes you think you'd have one now?"

Reggie whipped around in his seat, eyes furious. "Mother—"

Tap, tap, tap.

There was a knock at the driver's door. Ronnie looked out and saw Devon.

Pastor Clayton rolled down the window. "What's up, Officer?"

"Just checking on you, Chief. Having car trouble?"

"No, just having a chat."

The pastor was about to roll up the window when Devon stopped him. "It's just that you turned off the main road with a prisoner who just assaulted you. All the tension with police relations right now, I don't want anyone getting in trouble. I want to make sure we, as a police community, take care of things."

The pastor smirked and nodded as Devon continued. "Tell you what, let me take her in for you."

Reggie sneered at Ronnie in the rearview mirror then looked back at Devon. "Take her. I'm not even sure how, but she's making my diabetes act up." He turned to Ronnie. "The sooner you leave town, the better."

Devon let her out of the car and Reggie drove off, kicking up dust in their faces. She stood still as Devon uncuffed her.

"Are you okay?"

"I'm fine. How's Rue?"

"I'm not sure. Chief Stevens is with her. I left not long after the two of you did. I didn't want you out here by yourself with him. The chief is retiring at the end of the year, and Reggie is slowly turning the department into a dictatorship."

"I did notice he seemed more smug than usual. Someone needs to teach him a lesson."

"Ronnie, look at me. Things are fine here. All you have to do is get in your car, go back home, and this will all be over."

"Dev, just take me to my car. If it makes you feel any better, I'm a whole grown woman in these streets with far too much to lose to be worried about Reggie Clayton's sorry ass."

15
THE PRICE OF AMBITION

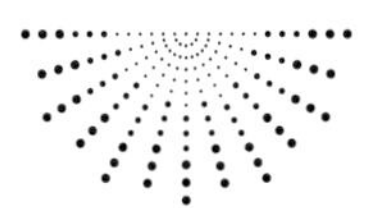

"How much for the nine millimeter?" Ronnie asked the vendor at the gun convention. After her run in with Reggie yesterday, she's decided to never allow herself to be put in that position again. Luckily for her, there was always a gun show in town. Everyone was a firm believer of the second amendment.

Since her outburst, Reggie had made it known he wanted her out of town, but she wasn't going anywhere. The thought of seeing her older sister being manipulated by their almost-stepfather infuriated her. Even though their family squabbles were far from over, Rue was her sister. Protecting her was Ronnie's priority after all she'd just been through.

Since Rue is clearly incapable of taking care of herself right now. I'll have to handle this. She thought.

"That one is $600," the vendor said as she examined the weapon.

Reggie was a trained police officer, but he was also arrogant. He never carried his gun off-duty. He thought he was untouchable, and he was mostly right. Everyone either respected, or was intimidated by, Reggie Clayton. It was hard not to, at six foot three, two hundred and fifty pounds of solid muscle back in his prime. He was still in good shape for his age and, though he had less muscle, he understood how to use his size. To make matters worse, it was a known fact that he would take over the police force when Chief Stevens retired; soon he'd have a congregation and the full weight of the police force at his disposal.

I may hate this place but I can't let this man be a tyrant, not in Momma's town.

She picked up another pistol. "How much is this one?"

"It's $650, not including rounds. An excellent weapon for a petite woman like yourself."

Ronnie smirked coyly. "I'd forgotten how charming southern men can be."

She was almost certain the middle-aged man was undressing her with his eyes. "If you're looking for a gun, you can't go wrong with the Glock .43. It's the perfect size."

"I'm looking for something to blow a motherfucker's head off. Will this do the trick?" she asked.

The vendor smiled brightly. "You come with some spice. I like it. I'll do it for five hundred, flat."

She shook the man's hand, and he turned around and rummaged through the metal sliding drawers behind him. After a spell, he turned around and handed her the weapon. She picked it up, testing the weight. It felt good in her hands.

"Do you have training?"

"I have enough." Learning to shoot was one of the first things she'd done when she left town. She fancied herself a decent shot.

She handed him back the weapon. "So, $500 for the gun and another $150 for the ammo. What about tax?"

"There's no tax on your second amendment right. Hell, I'd give it to you for free if I could afford it."

Ronnie reached into her purse and pulled out seven crisp hundred-dollar bills. "Keep the change. For the cause."

"Right on, sister!" the old man nodded in agreement as he handed her the bag with the bullets, and wiped down the gun for her to carry. Like everybody else in this neck of the woods, this patriot had a vendetta against Big Government.

As she left the gun show, her phone rang.

Doug – Assistant.

She answered the call. "Doug, what have you found out?"

"Ms. Duvalle, I'd like to say something, if I may."

"Go ahead."

"First, I want you to know how much I appreciate you fighting for my job. I love it here, and I love working for you. You're such an inspi—"

"Land the plane, Doug."

"Right, I'm sorry. What I'm trying to say is, I'm thankful for my job, but I'm not sure if I approve of the things I've been made to do as of late."

"Such as?"

"Well, for starters, the commercial, and, if I'm being honest, some of what I had to do to get this information."

"Doug, you work at the most powerful company in the fourth largest city in the country. Do you know why we hire our administrative assistants from Harvard, Yale, and Rice, instead of using a temp agency?"

"Well, I assume beca—"

"That was rhetorical. You already know the answer; we need the best and most capable minds giving us real-time answers to critical questions. The people at your level who leave this firm go on to make six figures for the rest of their lives. Do you know what strings I had to pull to keep you here?"

"I know, and I truly app— "

"Again, rhetorical. Don't think for one second that your Ivy League education will keep you where I've placed you. I'm your only protector. Study under me and when you leave, you can write your own ticket. A rising tide lifts all boats, Doug. We're in this together. You're running with lions now, and this is how the pride hunts."

Doug stammered, "You're right... I'm sorry. I'll do anything to prove myself to this company."

"Doug, the company wasn't loyal to you, I was. Prove yourself to me and you'll have nothing to worry about."

"You're right. Sorry. Well, regarding the information I found. Pastor Reginald Clayton is almost $600,000 in debt. There's a loan on the church, and he doesn't have any liquid assets. He's selling a house to cover some of it, but needs to make a balloon payment of $438,000 in two days or he loses everything."

"Wait, you said he's selling a house?"

"Yes, owned by Reggie and Vanessa Clayton."

"Was there an owner before that?"

"Yes, a Vicki Duvalle."

"Son of a... Thanks Doug, I'll call you back."

Ronnie got in her car and started for the rehab center when her phone rang again. She didn't recognize the number, but it was a Houston area code.

She connected the call via Bluetooth. "This is Ronnie."

"Well played, Ms. Duvalle. Well played, indeed," Martin Burrows praised.

"Martin, I can't say I'm surprised to hear from you. I take it, you saw my little interview?"

"I did. Tell me, how did you get to be so clever?"

"Well, Martin, not all bitches take well to a whack on the nose. Some of us bite back."

"It would appear so. I'm a pragmatist, Ms. Duvalle, so I have no problem admitting you've put me in a bind. Even if I wanted to, I can't fire or demote you. The board would have a collective aneurysm. Any unfortunate 'accident' or illness would look suspicious as well."

"All true, Martin," Ronnie gleefully chimed in, pleased to know her plan had its desired outcome.

"There's also the dilemma of addressing the notion that we don't hire nig—excuse me, *minorities* beyond the vice presidency of my company."

"Careful, Martin, your white sheet is showing," Ronnie quipped.

"And since you're the highest-ranking, longest-tenured Black executive, it would seem that I have no choice but to promote you, the person who caused this shitstorm. It makes sense; you have a proven track record, and are directly responsible for the rise – and fall – of our stock recently."

"I'm glad we're seeing eye to eye on this, Martin," Ronnie responded, her plan playing out perfectly.

"My dear, I didn't get this far in life by being backed into corners. You are going to want to turn the news and watch *Invest Talk*."

Ronnie pulled over and opened up a streaming platform on her phone, pulling up the cable news channel.

She watched as Milton Burrows walked up to the podium.

"We at Burrows Industries are aware of the insensitive nature of our ill-advised ad. While we did not properly vet it, we searched deep in our company's collective moral compass to see if there was any truth to the portrayal. What we discovered is that we practice what we preach in terms of diversity. A staggering 63 percent of our firm is made up of women, people of color and those who identify as LGBTQ+. But the message we want to send to our country and investors is that we can always do better, especially at the top level."

Milton paused as the cameras flashed, taking a moment to clear his throat.

"That is why, effective immediately, we are promoting Kendra Daniels to the role of Marketing Senior Vice President to ensure that commercials like this are never made again.

"This is not for our shareholders. Kendra has proven herself to be a valuable asset to this company, and I know she will do remarkable things for our company in her new role. For now I'd like to invite Kendra Daniels up to speak."

The news hit Ronnie like an avalanche. She felt queasy, but was careful not to give any hint of anger to Martin, who was still on the call. She watched as Kendra stepped on stage.

"Thank you, Milton. When I was offered this position, I was initially hesitant. If I'm being honest, I thought it was a knee-jerk reaction to the commercial debacle, and I didn't want to be the 'diversity hire' to prove to the public that the company isn't racist.

"But then I took the time to think about what Mr. Burrows spoke about just now, and I met his father, the legendary Martin Burrows.

He sat me down and told me he'd been following my career closely, and I had his full support to bring about any changes I see fit to help us connect with our customers. We're doing this for our customers. Because this is how Burrows Industries responds to adversity: with more diversity. Thank you all."

Ronnie squeezed the phone to the point her nails chipped off. Martin chimed in and said,

"Like I said, it was a nice try. When you get back, you'll report directly to Ms. Daniels. While you're processing your failure, I'd like to tell you what happened to my dear old collie."

Ronnie sat silently on the phone, still in shock.

"One night, after a long day of trying to steal apples, she fell into a ravine and broke both her hind legs. My father couldn't afford to pay the vet to help her mend, so he looked me in my eyes and said, 'Son, we have to put the bitch down.'"

"Well, congratulations, Martin, you won the pissing contest. You have proven beyond a shadow of a doubt that you are the biggest dick in the room. I guess the only question now is, how long can you keep it up?"

Before he could respond, she hung up the phone. She wasn't sure if Martin knew of her rivalry with Kendra, and she didn't care.

Before she even had time to comprehend the call with Martin, her phone shrilled again.

"Right on cue," she huffed as she answered her phone. "Hey girl, Congratulations." Her heart wanted to scream at Kendra, but she fought to keep her voice professional.

Never let them see you sweat.

She listened quietly as Kendra got her thoughts together. "I wanted to tell you. I mean, I was trying to call, but you didn't answer the phone and—"

"Nothing to call me about, Kendra. You did your thing, and the right people noticed. Congratulations."

"Ronnie...look, I know this is hard. We're both equally qualified for this position, but you know I don't make the rules—"

"Kendra, it's fine. You don't have to worry about my feelings; that don't pay the bills. I'm happy for you."

She wasn't happy at all. She knew Kendra had to feel some satisfaction at beating her out. All of Ronnie's calculated moves to get the position, and she still missed it. There was nothing she could do at the moment but live with it.

"Ronnie, you know I got you, right?"

"Kendra, I'm a grown woman. I got myself. But thank you."

"I didn't mean—"

"I know what you meant, and I appreciate it. Look, I'm in the middle of something. Can I call you back? Maybe we can do lunch now that you're gonna be back in town, telling me what to do."

There was silence on the phone.

She had done the one thing she'd never done since she'd known Kendra: shown her cards. There could be no question she was pissed.

"Okay, Ronnie, I'll let you go. When you're ready to talk, I'm available."

"Thanks, girl. Take care now." She threw her phone against the dashboard in frustration. All of the emotions of the last few weeks flowed out of her, done with being suppressed.

"Son of a bitch!"

16
UNLOVEABLE

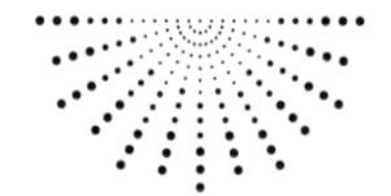

Rue turned off the water for the tub and stepped in, immediately calm.

Finally alone.

With her aunt and surrogate mother, Van, in rehab, and Reggie and Ronnie hauled off, she had no one around. She'd given the staff the day off because she wanted peace to sit with her thoughts.

Her favorite playlist played in the background, one her late husband, Malcolm, made for her in better days. When her favorite song, Don't Disturb This Groove by The System, came on, she shimmied in the tub as she sipped a strong whiskey, singing to the music.

After an hour-long soak, she dunked her head then hopped out. Her reflection in the mirror caught her eye as she dried off, and she remembered the days she didn't feel pretty.

She was considerably darker than her sister – which is how she got the nickname Rue, referencing the color of gumbo roux. It had bothered her when she was younger, but not anymore. She'd grown extremely comfortable with herself; she loved her skin.

She finished drying off and got dressed, then grabbed her journal to explore her feelings. As she was about to sit down to write, she heard the doorbell. She hopped up and walked over to open the door.

"Devon! Come in. What brings you over?" she asked.

Devon walked in the door. "Hey Rue, is Ronnie here?"

"No, she left a while ago. Something about going to a gun show? But I'm glad you stopped by. I need your help with something."

"Sure, what's up?"

"I've got this pistol I've been wanting to use for target practice, but the darn target is in a hard spot for me to reach."

"Okay, you want me to get it for you? Where's the target?"

"It's right here." Rue grabbed his hand, placing it on her crotch.

Devon smiled and kissed her passionately, slapping her ass cheek.

Rue yelped and giggled. "So, Detective, are you going to help me reach the target and...Dick'em Down?"

Devon let her go with a groan. "She told you?"

"We're sisters, Dev. Even when we're not talking, we're talking."

"This isn't a thing."

"Oh, it's already a thing, Triple D."

Devon pulled Rue in to kiss her again. "If you weren't so damn sexy, I'd leave right now. Wait, you didn't tell her about us, did you?"

"No, and I don't plan on it."

"But you just said—"

"Devon, my sister is gone for who knows how long. We can either continue this conversation, or you can spend it firing as many rounds as you can muster inside of me, but we only have time for one."

Devon raised his hand like a schoolkid with the correct answer. "I'll take what's behind door number two, please."

She pulled his head down to hers for a passionate kiss.

Arms under her ass, Devon lifted Rue and took her into the office, closing the door behind him. He tossed her haphazardly on the couch and unbuttoned his pants. As soon as he pulled his boxers down, Rue pulled the tip of his dick into her mouth.

"Damn, I've missed you," she said, looking at his hardening dick. She slowly teased him by sucking and kissing it.

Devon moaned in anticipation.

Rue then took the entire shaft as far as she could, until she nearly gagged on his now-throbbing dick.

"That feels good, baby," he moaned. Devon looked at her as she stuck her tongue out. He slapped his dick on her tongue until she grabbed it and began stroking it with both hands.

"Want me to put my mouth on it?" she asked seductively.

Devon nodded, and Rue inhaled his manhood. "Damn, Rue, you're not playing today," he moaned.

She smiled around his length.

Devon's dick was pulsing, ready to explode, when she pulled away from him.

"My turn."

"But I was nearly there. Just finish it for me, please," he begged.

Rue stood up and slipped off her house clothes, laying across the couch. "My turn," she repeated.

Playfully, Devon got on his knees and grumbled, "Shoot, you talk about Ronnie being selfish, when you're the selfish one."

"Boy, shut up and come taste me."

Rue shoved his face into her pussy.

Devon went right to the spot he'd been learning for the last three months, forcing a moan of ecstasy from Rue.

"Lick it, baby…just like that," she moaned as Devon inhaled her, forcing her moisture to build.

"Oh damn, baby, that feels incredible. Eat that pussy," she whispered. "I-I'm…oh God!"

Her orgasm saturated the bristles of his mustache and dripped to his chin.

As she laid there panting, she looked at him lustfully and said, "You know what I want."

Devon stood up and grabbed her by the back of her head, shoving his dick as far as he could into her throat. As Rue gagged, she gripped his thighs and pulled him in further.

"Fuck!" he moaned.

As she pulled his dick out of her mouth, she watched the saliva drip from the tip. Rue slurped the saliva up and spit it back out on his dick.

She stroked it for good measure and stood up, turning around.

"You're hard enough now. I'm ready."

Without hesitation, Devon slid his dick inside of her, and she gasped in pleasure as he set a hard and steady pace.

After several thrusts, he moaned, "Oh, I feel you opening up. You want me deep in that thang today."

"Take it, daddy. Take it," she moaned as Devon pounded her pussy without regard. The harder he fucked her, the louder she begged for it. It wasn't long before she was screaming, "Oh shit, I'm cumming!"

She began to orgasm, making her already warm, wet pussy too much for Devon to handle. With a few more strokes, he asked, "Do you want it?"

"I need it, daddy."

"Just stay right there. I'm about to give it to you." Devon released his seed deep into her walls. He moaned savagely, pumping his dick until his cum spilled out of her sweet, wet pussy.

The pair fell to the couch in the office and looked at each other, bursting into laughter. Devon kissed Rue, grabbing hold of her hand. "Hey, I know how things ended yesterday with Ronnie wasn't ideal. Are you two good?"

"We're fine. Why would I be mad at her? She's always been selfish. I'm mad at myself for thinking she'd react any other way. But we worked it out."

"That's good. We both know how she can be a bit…well, Ronnie. But I gotta tell you, the other day I came over and she was about to leave town. We had a friendly talk, and after a while I realized she was different."

"What do you mean?"

"She's…lighter, if that makes sense. Even in her sadness, she's happier. It's almost like she has this glow about her. I don't know, maybe that sounds stupid. But I know having her sister back in her life has to be part of it."

Rue cupped his cheek, rubbing her thumb in his beard. "Dev, you are so sweet and so very stupid. The only reason she was glowing is because she's pregnant."

Devon's eyes widened as he sat up. "She's what?"

Realizing her mistake, Rue sat up as well. "Devon Flynn, you can *not* tell her I told you that."

"Why would you think I'd say any—"

"Because you're a blabbermouth."

He smirked. "You never have a problem when that mouth is on your you-know-what."

She threw her head back in laughter. "I never said I had a problem with it, just that you talk too much." Devon shrugged as he rolled his eyes as Rue playfully bit him on his shoulder, after a spell he finally responded.

" Well it doesn't matter anyway she already told me."

"Then why did you preten—"

"Because I knew you didn't think I could keep a secret. I just wanted to know if you knew. Ronnie's gonna always be my friend. So we may not talk on the levels of sisterhood. But it's close."

"That's fair."

"And I'm not a blabbermouth. I just don't like to keep secrets from the people I care about. Hell, I still think we should tell Ronnie about us."

Rue leaned into him, resting her head against his shoulder. "Dev, we can't tell anyone about us. If word got out at the church that we'd been carrying on like this before Malcolm died...I don't think I could live with the scrutiny."

"I know, but when is there ever gonna be an appropriate time to tell them you're my woman?"

"I'm your woman?"

"Yeah, you kno—"

"No, I'm *my* woman. No one will ever have dominion over me again."

There was an awkward silence. Rue could tell she'd hurt his feelings. She sat up on the couch and looked into his eyes. "Devon, baby, listen to me. I've been married a long time and, while I have needs, I just want to keep it fun, you know? You've been such a comfort, and you make me think brighter days are coming. But I loved my husband.

What we're doing isn't easy. What you're asking of me right now is just gonna make it harder."

"I understand. I didn't mean to make you feel like I wanted to control you or anything. It's just...the last three months have felt like a dream. Like I found a woman that I want to tell the world about. I know right now I could spend the rest of my life waking up and looking at your smile."

"And cooking for me, because you know I love your gumbo," she giggled.

"And yes, cooking for you. It's funny you say that..." Devon laid back down on the couch, and Rue rested her head on his chest. "I learned how to make gumbo because of you."

"What? You're gonna have to explain that one."

Devon kissed her on the forehead. "When I first met you, I thought you were the most beautiful thing this side of the Mississippi. I asked Miss Hinderwell who you were, and she said, 'Those are the Duvalle girls. The light one is Veronica and the darker one is Valerie.' You remember how proper she was."

"Oh, that sounds just like her," Rue laughed at Devon's impression.

"It took me another three days to find out everyone called you Rue. That's how me and Ronnie became friends."

"Devon, don't lie."

"Ask her. I'm serious."

"Let's say that's true. It still doesn't explain how you learned to make gumbo so damn good."

"Well, my senior year. I wanted to ask you to prom, so my plan was to make you the best gumbo in the world. Must have made a roux about fifty times before I got it right. And then made it all winter long. By crawfish season, I was ready. So, I made the gumbo, and by now everyone knows how good I am, so Momma wanted me to enter the gumbo cook-off, and I did."

"You won it that year, right?"

"I was the runner-up that first year, then I won it three years in a row, but that's not the point. I entered knowing Pastor Clayton is gonna bring his family. I know y'all are gonna come by my booth, so my plan was to give you a card that said, 'I hope you like this roux I made for you. Gumbo is an art. It's beautiful, just like you. I learned how to do all of this to go to prom with you. Because my roux is tailor-made for Rue.'"

Rue smiled. "That is the sweetest thing ever. Why didn't you do that?"

"Cause Ronnie told me it was the dumbest thing she'd ever heard. She said I used the word 'you' too many times. The prom had nothing to do with gumbo; tons of holes in the plan."

"You know your friend is a sadist, right?"

"She's a piece of work. But also, that was the year y'all didn't come to the cookoff. Matter fact, you moved out that week."

"Oh, that week. Yeah, that was a rough time."

Devon kissed her on her forehead again. "Rue, I know we're in different spaces, but when I was a kid, I used to dream about what it would be like to be your boyfriend. And when I get off, I'm fantasizing about all the stuff we just did."

"You're so nast—"

"The point I'm trying to make is, I've loved you my whole life."

Rue was silent as Devon looked her in her eyes unwaveringly. She believed him. Without breaking eye contact, she asked, "Why are you telling me this now?"

"Like I said, I had a great talk with Ronnie. Seeing the changes in her made me want more for myself. It makes me want to see what I'm made of, not just as an officer, but as a man. Which is why I'll go ahead and tell you, I made detective, junior grade."

Rue's eyes lit up with excitement. "You passed the exam?"

"Yep, got my shield and all. Start today."

"That's great, Dev. I'm so proud of you."

"Thank you, Rue. You inspired me and pushed me. I know you're still grieving, but if the day ever comes when you want to try again, I'm here for you and I'm willing to wait as long as it takes."

Rue kissed him. "Okay, let's get cleaned up. I told the chief I'd show Sarah Ann how to make a carrot cake today."

"Why would you need to show Sarah Ann—"

"I already knew about your promotion, Dev. The chief told me about it a few days ago. I'm more than happy to make a cake for Detective Dick'em Down."

Devon took one of the throw pillows and threw it at her. "That will not become a thing!"

17

FORGIVENESS (PART I)

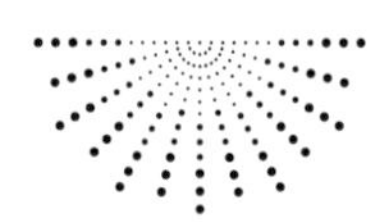

Having unleashed her emotions on the side of the road, Ronnie finally reached her destination and got out of the car, only to immediately fall to her knees and vomit.

"Goddamnit! This is all your fault!" she screamed to her stomach.

She instantly felt horrible, and fell to the pathway crying. One of the guards at the facility walked over to assist her. "Miss, do you need help?"

"I'm fine," she fired back.

She stood up and composed herself. Right now, she had to deal with her aunt, the last person she wanted to see.

Though she was still bothered at the way she'd yelled at the baby, she walked down the hallway to her aunt's room. Before she stepped in, she paused.

"I'm sorry," she whispered, rubbing her stomach.

She walked into the room and spotted her aunt sitting by the window smoking a cigarette. "Did you get any vomit on those expensive clothes of yours?"

"No, Van, I didn't."

"Too bad. So, you gonna get rid of it or what?"

Ronnie admitted the truth. "I thought about it. Until just now, I wasn't sure. Primarily because...well, I'm fucked up. I'm not cut out to be a mother."

"Ain't that the truth?" Van took a drag of her cigarette and chuckled.

"But it was right out there when I decided I'm going to keep the baby. Because no matter how fucked up I am, I can't ever be worse than you.

Vanessa ashed the cigarette onto the floor. "You think you're hot shit, don't you? Coming in here, with your designer clothes and purse—"

"Why don't we both save ourselves the time? I have everything you always wanted but couldn't have. And why couldn't you have it?"

"'Cause I got saddled with you after Vicki went off and killed herself."

"Well, I'm sorry, Van! I'm sorry I was born. I'm sorry Reggie's got you so brainwashed that you see the worse in your own flesh and blood, and I'm sorry you got saddled with two kids you never wanted. Like it or not, you were the only mom we had, and I'm sorry we made your life a living hell, but we lost our real momma, so just take a minute to imagine what kind of hell our life was like."

Silence filled the room. Van picked up another cigarette as Ronnie continued. "I'm done holding on to resentment, Van. I'm done holding onto the painful memories of this hellhole of a city. I won't be coming back here. And I want to let you know something: I forgive you."

"Oh, here we go, ladies and gentlemen. Miss High and Mighty, all the way from the big city, about to bat them big green eyes while she looks down on us."

"Let me finish, please. I forgive you. I love you as much as I do my actual mother. But you are not my mother, Auntie Van. My mother's name was Vicki Duvalle. You can call me crazy – you can call me anything else – but we are going to talk about her. I'm going to live the life she wanted for me, and for Rue. Despite your cruelest moments, and your absences, she wanted good things for you too. You miss your sister. Like I've missed mine." She began to tear up. She wiped her tears and continued.

"Look, this is all we got as a family. We're not the Huxtables – we're not even the Evans', but we're here. It's time to move forward. We should bury the hatchet. I used to always wonder why I would hurt everyone around me, and it's because all I ever saw in our house was hurt, and pain, and fighting, to the point where it's all I know how to do. Well, I'm done.

"My baby daddy as you like to call him, hasn't given me one single reason to push him away, which is what I was doing, thinking of not keeping his child. And why? Because I'm a rotten apple from a rotten tree, and because we don't talk about shit in this family. We just hold it in. All the pain, all the suffering, all the fucked-up shit that goes on, and we don't say one word. We don't talk about your drug addiction. We don't talk about our real momma, and above all else, we don't talk about Reggie Clayton!"

"Now you shut your damn mouth! I will kick your high, yellow ass if you—"

"If I what, Van? Call your husband a hoe? A womanizer? An alcoholic? a gambler? Or should I call him by his real name?"

"You little whore, you hush your fucking mouth! I'm warning you!"

"A lying, power-hungry, dirty cop pretending to be a servant of the Lord—"

Crack.

Vanessa slapped Ronnie with all her might. "I don't give a damn what you have to say! He is my husband! He's an officer of the law, and you will show some respect."

Ronnie cut her eyes to Vanessa as she held her face. "Where is he then, Van? When's the last time he came to see you in here? When's the last time he treated you like a wife?"

"Ronnie, shut the fuck up! I mean it!" Vanessa screamed at the top of her lungs.

"No, I won't shut up. This is the first time you've been sober since I can remember, so I'm gonna say it: fuck Reggie Clayton. He is a monster! I know it, Rue knows it – hell, even you would see it if you weren't so damn high all the time. He's had so many babies outside of your marriage, I've lost count. We had a nickname for them; instead of Pastor's kids, we called them Clayton's kids."

"Ronnie, you don't know what you're talking about."

"Oh, cut the shit, Van. The other day at the funeral I saw a cute little boy, couldn't have been but five years old, and my first thought was, *there's another C.K.* He's been doing this for years, and you know it."

"Ronnie, you—"

"No, I'm here for the truth, Van, and the truth is, the world would be a better place if he wasn't in it anymore. And before you quote the Bible, let me remind you, that's the only place God has ever lived, because he damn sure was never in our house."

Vanessa stood up, the cigarette smoke she puffed a fitting metaphor for the tension in the room. "So, you wanna take the gloves off? Fine. I can give as good as I get. You, Ronnie Duvalle, are an evil little girl. From the time you were born we all knew it. Your birth was a curse on this whole family – that's why Rodrick left your momma. The moment you were born, he knew you wasn't his kid. And from that moment, everything went to hell."

"I might be a curse, but at least I'm not haunted by the fact that I had to sleep with the man who helped cover up my sister's murder."

"Ronnie, you were five years old. You don't know what the hell you're talking about."

"The man is a monster, and you know it. I told you exactly what happened, and you let him come in there and discredit me."

"You were a kid."

"I saw what I saw! And I told you! My aunt, the only person in the world who could've done something about it, did nothing. The longer you stayed silent, the more it ate at all of us." Vanessa slammed her hand against the wall and screamed.

"Where was I going to go, Ronnie?! I'm an infertile woman raising my sister's two kids who hate me, in a podunk town, with no education or skills. Who would want me? What was I gonna do, huh? Answer me the fuck that? What was I gonna do? I didn't have the chance to get a formal education, like Vicki, or Rue, or even you."

"You could've gone to Chief Stevens and—"

"Chief Stevens has his head so far up Reggie's ass, he knows what he ate for breakfast!" Van said. "The night Vicki died, I went to Reggie. I told him what you told me, and you know what he said?"

"What?"

"He said, 'Keep your goddamn mouth shut' and so I did, because what else was I gonna do?" she said. Vannessa began to sob and then continued."I worked in a goddamn meat plant, making less than minimum wage because my momma – your grandmother – got sick and someone had to support this family." Van threw the pack of cigarettes at Ronnie in frustration. When they hit the ground, she picked up the pack off the ground and pulled one out.

jealous

After a couple of drags of the cigarette, she continued. "I had dreams too – big dreams. I wanted to be a singer. I used to go down to the Red Rooster and sing all night. That was my gift. But all anyone ever cared about was Vicki. Light skinned, good hair Vicki. She was beautiful, like you, and just as selfish – hell, probably even more so. She wanted to go to college and because 'singing don't pay no bills', my dreams would have to wait. I had to do everything I could to help her get through school.

"You think Reggie was bad? Those men at that meat plant were real sons of bitches. I was barely alive, the way they treated me. But I endured it for my momma, for Vicki, and even for you two. Those white boys would try to have their way with me; as far as they were concerned, I was just another piece of meat at the factory." She folded her arms and looked off in the distance, lost in a memory.

"One night, one of my co-workers got drunk and wanted more than what was on the menu. He caught me walking home and tried to... I said no and before I knew it, he hit me over the head with a bottle and pushed me down to the ground. I still remember the scent of bourbon on his breath when he said, 'you finna have some white meat tonight, you uppity black bitch'. I tried to fight him, but I could barely feel my legs after the crack over the skull. He had me pinned down so hard I still have scars on my wrist, he hit me till I had no fight left in me. After I tried to bite him, he choked me to within an inch of my life. I was just gonna give up and let him have his way when Officer Reggie Clayton showed up." owe him

Vanessa smiled, and a tear rolled from her eye. "He jumped out of his police car and beat that white boy to within an inch of his life. I mean, this strong, handsome black man was just knocking this white boy around the parking lot, and no one said a word, because he was police. He did it for me; not Vicki, but Vanessa Duvalle, the ugly one. You'll never know what that meant to me. Vanessa began to shake and took a breath to compose herself as she continued.

"It wasn't long after that we got married, and those were some of the best days of my life. Reggie was thoughtful; he was going places, and he cared about me. I loved that man. Before I knew it, I was the first lady of Mount Ebenezer Baptist and everyone knew me."

She put out the last of the cigarette and lit another. "And then Vicki came back to town. Her and Rodrick were happy for a while, just them two and Rue, but Vicki wanted the city life. Rodrick just wanted a farm.

"When she came back from college and was pregnant with you, it tore him up inside, the fact Vicki had been with someone else. He was never the same, and neither was she. Vicki started partying, drinking, using any man she could find to keep her warm at night. She was an absolute wreck. I tried to give her support. Hell, I tried to get her to come to this place, because she needed it. But you don't remember that about your momma. All you remember is sweet Vicki Duvalle just like everyone else. So yeah, when Reggie told me she committed suicide and to shut the hell up, I did just that."

Ronnie walked over to her surrogate mother and held both of her hands.

"Like I said, I forgive you." She kissed her on the cheek and turned around to walk out of the door.

Before making it out the door, she turned back for one last comment. "Your husband will need to find another way to pay off his debts. I'm going to do everything I can to keep my mom's house. In fact, I've already got a petition in place to stop the sale, and before you act like you don't know what I'm talking about, I know you know he's in debt big. Tell him or don't, it doesn't matter. Goodbye, Momma."

Ronnie walked out of the door and got in her car.

Van's admission had hurt, but in the end, it didn't matter. Her life was in Houston now. There was just one more place she needed to go before she left town.

18
DAUGHTERS

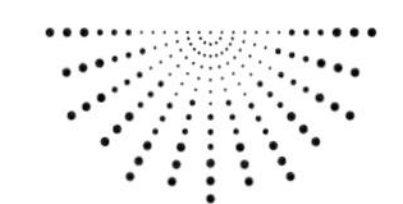

"I'm serious, when can I see you again?" Devon asked over the phone.

Rue smiled as she drove. "I'm gonna see you today when I get to the station."

"You know what I'm talking about. I want more."

"You're never satisfied, Devon, but luckily, you're adorable. I'm gonna check when Ronnie is leaving. If she's already gone, you can come back later."

"That's what I'm talking about. Okay, baby, I gotta go. We got a meeting."

"Okay Detective junior grade, I'll see you soon," Rue said as she hung up the phone.

She smiled as she imagined Devon's powerful sexual energy engulfing her. It had been years since she'd been with another man. Malcolm had been too sick to have sex, and she'd been too emotionally drained to think about it. Devon had been a breath of fresh air the past few months.

As she turned onto the back road Chief Stevens lived on, she quickly slowed down, spotting a familiar teenager walking down the street, trembling and cuddling herself.

Rue pulled up next to the girl and parked the car. When she stepped out and walked over, her suspicions were confirmed.

"Sarah Ann! Are you alright? What happened?"

The teenager was shivering, and had clearly been crying. Her shirt had a tear in it, and her knees were scuffed.

Rue approached the teen and embraced her. "Shhhh. It's going to be okay. Just tell me what happened."

Sarah Ann kept quiet.

Rue ushered her to the passenger seat of her car and rounded the car, making a quick U-turn to drive to the police station. Sarah was silent the entire ride.

Rue put her hand on the girl's shoulder. "It's gonna be okay, honey, I promise."

When they arrived at the police station, Rue parked the car and ran inside, looking for the chief. As fate would have it, he was standing at the reception desk speaking to an officer.

"Chief Stevens. Do you have a moment?"

"Hi Rue, if you're looking for Reggie, he's not—"

"I'm not here for Daddy, Chief Stevens. I need to talk to you… about a personal matter."

"Sure, what's this about?"

"Can we talk some place… a little more private?"

"Now, Rue, I don't have a lot of ti—"

"It's about Sarah Ann."

The chief was shocked silent. He turned to the officer he was talking to. "Lorraine, this will only take a second," he said.

He led Rue to his office and swiftly closed the door.

He approached her, standing so close she could feel his breath on her face. He put both hands on her shoulders lightly, then held her firmly. "Rue, I need you to be straight with me now. Is my daughter in trouble?"

Rue was quiet until Chief Stevens shook her gently. "Rue!"

"That's the thing, Chief, I don't know."

"Where is she?"

Rue took a deep breath as she said a quick prayer. "I…I found her walking down Hester Street. She looks like she'd been in a fight or something, but she won't talk to me. She's outside in my car. I didn't want to bring her in and make a scene or anything. From what I can tell, she's alright physically, but—"

"Did somebody hurt my little girl?"

"That's not for me to say. I just brought her here in the hopes that she'd talk to you, but please stay calm, Chief. She's already feeling apprehensive."

Chief Stevens became flushed and, after a few moments, uttered, "You did good, Rue. Where is she now?"

"Outside…in my car."

The chief put his hands on his head and took a deep breath. "Okay, hurry and bring her around back. I'll open the door for you."

Rue nodded and quickly returned to the car. The young girl was still seated in the front, quiet and afraid.

She opened the driver-side door and turned the car on. "It's gonna be alright, darlin', your daddy is waiting for us."

Sarah Ann nodded her head as Rue pulled up behind the police station, not taking the time to look for a parking space. She parked at the door, exited the car, and guided Sarah Ann into the police station, where her father was anxiously awaiting them.

"Pumpkin, are you okay? What happened to you?" Chief Stevens demanded.

Sarah Ann refused to answer, still trembling.

Rue watched the chief's temper rise. "Did somebody hurt you? Was it one of the boys at school?"

The girl continued to stay quiet.

"Chief, I reckon it's best we take this in your office."

The chief agreed and led them through the precinct. When they made it behind closed doors, the line of questioning continued.

"Sarah Ann, sweetheart, tell me what happened?"

Still no answer. The stillness made his temper worse. "Goddamn it, sweetheart, talk to me!"

The chief slammed his fist into a wall, the commotion causing a couple of officers to run into the room.

"Hey, Chief, is everything okay?" one officer asked.

"I'm fine! Everything is fine. Just get back to work."

Rue put her hands around Sarah Ann's shoulders to comfort her.

Chief's scrubbed both hands over his face in frustration.

"Chief, should we call your wife?" Rue suggested.

"She's out of town. Rue, just what in the hell happened?"

"I know as much as you know. I was on my way to pick up Sarah Ann to make the cake we talked about, and I found her like this. She wasn't too far from Lake Martin. I'm sorry, I wish there was more I could say or do, but I wasn't there."

"It's not your fault, Rue. Thank you for bringing her to me."

She watched as he diverted his attention back to his daughter, his training as a police officer taking over. "Now, Sarah Ann, I tell you all the time I work hard, so you never have to worry about the bad guys. I know you're scared, but if we're gonna catch this son of a bitch, we need you to remember what I taught you about memory recall. Close your eyes and describe for me everything you can remember. Can you do that for me, pumpkin?"

Rue watched the Chief, on the verge of tears, calm his fiery anger. She wanted to console both him and Sarah, so she began to pray.

Sarah Ann finally broke her silence. "He was black. Over six feet tall."

Chief Stevens placed his hands on his daughter's shoulders. "Good girl, just breathe. Did he hurt you?"

"No. He tried, but he got scared and ran off."

"Okay, now we're getting somewhere. Did he have any identifiable marks?"

The girl shook her head dismissively.

Rue tapped the Chief on his shoulder. "Hey Chief, this feels like a family matter. Maybe I should go."

"No Rue, stay. Any little detail can be helpful," the chief pleaded.

As she nodded in agreement, Sarah Ann spoke again. "He smelled."

"What do you mean?"

"I don't know, he just smelled."

"Like what? Catfish? Crawfish? Sweat from the gym?"

"No, like cologne…it was really strong. I don't know, Daddy. I'm sorry."

The man hugged his daughter. "It's okay, you did good, pumpkin. I'm just glad you're alright. We're gonna find the bastard who did this and we're gonna make him pay. You have my word."

The chief walked over to the hallway where a few officers were eavesdropping. "Can one of you be useful and get me a sketch artist to work on Sarah Ann's description? Where the hell is Devon?"

"He's still in the meeting."

"I need you to call the whole goddamn force in. I don't care what they're doing. An attack on one of us is an attack on all of us, and no one sleeps until we get this son of a bitch off the streets, you hear me?"

A chorus of "Yes, sir!" rang out.

Chief Stevens turned back to Rue. "When you found her, was there anything out of the ordinary? Anything you can think of?"

"I told you all I know."

"Think harder. I need answers!"

An officer approached them, looking sheepish. "Chief, the sketch artist is on vacation."

Fury overtook the chief's expression. "Are you kidding me?"

"You approved it last we—"

"She's fired. Get me someone from another county, right now, or you'll be next!"

"Will do, sir, but you have to remain calm."

"You don't tell me to goddamn calm down when someone tried to assault my daughter!"

"Chief!" Rue yelled.

She pulled him to the side. "I understand you're upset, but you gotta set a good example for your men. Let's go somewhere a little more private."

Chief Stevens nodded, and they walked with Sarah Ann into the closest room, which happened to be Reggie's office.

The door swung closed and they were once again alone, Reggie's scent overwhelming them in the dark room. The sound of water hitting the floor could be heard, and a rancid smell reached their nose.

Rue looked to Sarah Ann to see her eyes wide open in fear. She'd peed herself.

"The smell, daddy. This is what he smelled like!" she howled, running to her father. Chief Stevens wrapped her in his arms, overwhelmed by disbelief, apprehension, and anger.

He looked at the bottle of cologne and then to Rue. There was no denying who'd done this to his daughter.

"Chief, there's gotta be a mist—"

"Rue, thank you for bringing my daughter in. You don't know how much I appreciate it. But I'm gonna need your cell phone."

"Now, Chief, you need to think—"

"I'm not gonna do anything stupid. I'm just gonna talk. But I can't have you leave this room."

Rue stood her ground. "You can't ke—"

"You can stay in this room with Sarah Ann, or you can sit in a cell. Either way, I need your phone. Now!"

Finally Rue handed over her phone, still in disbelief.

The chief took the phone and walked out the door. "Officer Blane, I need you to guard this door. No one goes in or out until I get back."

"Yes, sir."

The chief locked the door and left.

why would you lock your daughter in there?

19
FORGIVENESS (PART II)

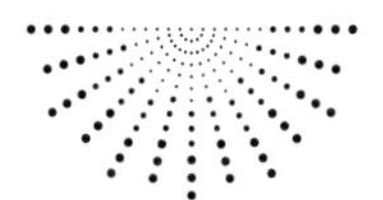

I guess this is as good a place as any.

Ronnie parked the car in front of the gravesite.

The conversation with Van made her realize it was high time to have a conversation with her actual mother. She was on the verge of an emotional breakdown – long-overdue since her mother died.

She felt raw; pain and confusion struck her like a baton in the pit of her stomach. She missed Vicki Duvalle so much. Her trip home had brought back so many memories of Vicki, and being pregnant only encouraged the thoughts.

So much was on her mind that she wanted to express.

As she walked to the gravesite, a haunting feeling overwhelmed her. It was the first day she'd visited the grave since her mother's funeral. She wondered if she would remember where the grave was, but her body knew the way – some things you can never forget. It was etched in her brain, like the moment she'd held the bloodied Tiffany box at her would-be proposal. It was a core memory.

A large, solid oak tree stood about twenty-five yards away from the grave, which was located on a slight hill. The grave markers ranged from round tombstones to sculptures of the Virgin Mary.

"Come on, girl, you got this," she pumped herself up.

Part of her wanted to jump in the car and head out of town. She was certain this would be the last time she'd ever return to her place of birth; it was a rare opportunity to be vulnerable.

She'd never gotten over losing her mother, and never would. She could recall sitting in a pool of blood trying to wake her mother up, even at the tender age of five. This was the place where Veronica had died and Ronnie Duvalle was born.

Taking a deep breath, she tenderly placed her hand on her stomach, shielding her unborn baby from the intense emotions that surged with each step. As she neared the cement tombstone, she was amazed to find it so well-maintained, undoubtedly one of the nicer ones in the vicinity - there were even fresh flowers in the flower holder. Typical Rue.

She had so much to say but couldn't figure out where to begin. She wanted to tell all of it to her.

She closed her eyes, took a deep breath, and kneeling on the trimmed grass, said, "Hey Momma."

Ronnie brought to mind the last image of her mother smiling, tears falling from her eyes.

"I don't know what to say to you. The pain is unbearable, Momma. I wish you were here with me. We could make some lemonade, and whip up some of those chocolate chip cookies, and then talk through all our worries. I wish I had that right now. These emotions are a son of a bitch."

She stopped to wipe away the tears and take a deep breath before speaking. "I guess I could start by saying I'm sorry I haven't come around to visit you. It's… well…I didn't want to come here ever again, honestly. But I'm in town, and I wanted to talk to you."

Ronnie shifted uncomfortably as she gazed at the headstone. She took a deep breath and proceeded. "I met someone. It wasn't part of my plan, but he's a nice person – a good person. He was gonna ask me to marry him, but, well... he's in the hospital. It's touch-and-go; it looks like we'll be getting married, or you could be meeting him sooner than I'm comfortable with. Either way, I'm gonna have his baby. Not only because he puts up with my bullshit, or because he's patient with me, but because I want to give this baby all the love you used to give me. Everybody deserves that."

The crying was uncontrollable now. Years of guarding her pain and anger came tumbling down.

She wiped her face and said with a smile, "I wish you were here. There's so much to talk about. Rue is still stuck in her bible; she needs you more than I do. Her husband died – you probably met him by now. I just saw Van; she's never let us forget she sacrificed everything for raising *your* kids. Blaming me and you for what happened. Hell, everyone blames us. But we know the truth. For so long, I blamed you for leaving us. I guess that's why I didn't come around, you know. Why I wanted to get out of town. But, Momma. I'm sorry. I'm so very sor—"

"She forgives you, Ronnie, and so does the Lord."

Shocked by the intrusion, she spun around to face Reggie Clayton, standing just feets away from her.

"You disrespectful maggot. You came to my mother's grave? Were you following me, you piece of shit? How dare you!" she screamed at the top of her lungs.

"Ronnie, look, we need to talk."

"And you pick here, of all places, to spew your venom? Fuck you!"

"Look Ronnie, I'll leave, I swear. But I *need* that money."

Ronnie laughed derisively. "I was wondering how long it would take for Vanessa to call you. You're a real sick piece of shit, you know that?"

"I don't care what you think about me, but I need that money, or your aunt won't have a—" ?

"I don't give a damn what you do with your wife."

She watched Reggie become enraged. "You know what your problem is, little girl? You don't know how to show respect – you never did. You've always been a hornet's nest. But you're going to show some damn respect. You're gonna let me sell that house or else—"

"Or what, Reggie? Just what in the good goddamn hell do you think you're gonna do to me? You think I'm scared of your little badge, or your little peashooter? Do you think you will ever have any kind of control over me again?"

Reggie stormed over to her. "You have lost your mind. I'm not fucking around with you, Ronnie!"

As he approached, Ronnie went into her purse and pulled out the pistol she'd purchased at the gun show and aimed it at Reggie, stopping him in his tracks. "I'm going to say this one time. Throw your gun on the ground."

"Bitch, do you know who you're dealing with? I'm Reggie motherfucking Clayton. I'll have your ass locked up before breakfast."

"Reggie, I came here for a lot of things. At the top of the list was closure. I can't think of a better form of closure than putting you in the ground. So, please, take one more step in my direction so I can blow your goddamn head off!"

Reggie slowly put his hands up in surrender, stepping toward her.

"Just remain calm, Ronnie. I think we want the same thing. You're going to shoot a cop in cold blood? Do you know how cops treat cop killers? You have a fancy career and life in a whole other city. I just want to make sure we can both go back to the lives we led before you came back into town."

"I don't give a shit what you want. You are a sorry excuse for a man. I don't give a fuck about your badge, and as you can see, I don't give a fuck about your gun. If you don't put your gun on the ground right now, I swear to god I'll do us all a favor and blow your motherfucking head off."

He took a moment to examine her – to gauge if she was exaggerating. "I'm not giving up my—"

Pop!

20

A TASTE OF DANGER

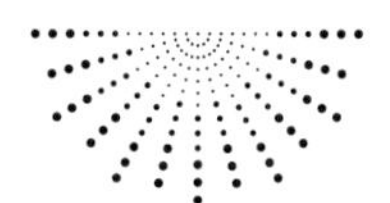

The bullet flew past Reggie's ear, hitting a tree behind him. He ducked then yelled in frustration.

"What in the hell is wrong with you?" he yelled, hastily throwing his gun on the ground.

Ronnie remained calm. "In case you're wondering, the first thing I did when I got to Houston was learn how to shoot. I missed on purpose. If you don't turn around and leave now, I won't miss again."

"I just need the money, Ronnie."

"You won't be getting that today, or ever. Now leave."

Reggie paused for a moment, then slowly backpedaled as he said. "All right, that's the way you want to play it, little girl? I'll be back. I'm getting my money."

She cocked the pistol again. "I swear to black Jesus, if you don't get out of here, I'm gonna put you in one of these plots. And don't you ever call me 'little girl' again."

He ran back toward the entrance. As he passed the tree holding her first bullet, he shouted back at her, "This ain't over, little girl!"

Pop, pop pop.

She fired off three more rounds.

Reggie scrambled towards his car and sped off.

She stood still, holding the gun, until she remembered she was at her mother's gravestone, and then the tears began flowing again. She let out a loud, uncontrollable wail and then fell to the ground at her mother's tombstone. The events of the past few days were too much for her.

Tears still wet on her face, she heard someone coming and assumed it was Reggie returning. Wiping the tears away, she grabbed her gun and rose, cocking it and pointing it at the blurry figure. "Don't you fucking move."

The man in front of her held his hands up in surrender. "Miss, I don't want any trouble. I just heard someone yelling and what sounded like gunshots. I'm just checking to see if anyone was hurt."

She was thankful it wasn't Reggie; just the groundskeeper. "I'm sorry, sir. I was—"

"Having a rough day?" Ronnie nodded in agreement and said.

"That obvious, huh?"

"It's gotta be a rough day if you need a pistol in a graveyard."

Ronnie laughed and became less tense, but she kept the gun in her grasp. "Yeah, I guess."

The groundskeeper lowered his hands. "Miss, do you need any help? Do you need me to call someone?"

Ronnie rose to her feet, looking around for Reggie. Seeing no sign of him, she put her gun away. "Thank you, but I'm fine."

"Well, I've never made it a habit to argue with someone holding a gun, but I don't think you're fine. In fact, I'd say you're far from it. It's none of my business why you have that gun, but I'd like to help you if you need it."

Ronnie studied the man. There was something about his honest nature and sincerity that reminded her of Walter Kimble, who's comfort she could really use right now. "Thank you. I was just having a moment. This is the first time I've been to my mother's grave."

The groundskeeper's eyes widened. He approached and softly touched her shoulder as she fought to keep control of her emotions. "Oh, I see. I'm sorry for your loss. I can imagine losing your mother is like losing everything."

His words broke Ronnie; she began to bawl.

The man embraced her, and she clutched onto him, weeping. "There, there. It's all gonna be okay, sweetie."

After a few minutes, she pulled away. "I'm sorry, I've just—"

"There is nothing to apologize for. Hell, I should apologize to you. You were having a private moment, and I interrupted it."

"It's fine, really."

"I just see a lot of grief in this place, and sometimes...well, if you can, you need to try to be there for people."

Ronnie gave a nod of approval. She felt at ease with him.

"Everyone around here calls me Duck. Listen, miss, if you want, I have coffee in the shed over there. It's not anything fancy, but I make a decent brew."

"I'd like that," she said.

Making sure to pocket Reggie's abandoned pistol, she adjusted her purse on her shoulder and let him guide her to the shed.

It was close by, and not in good condition. There were rusty wheelbarrows scattered around, as well as shovels, hoses, and bags of fertilizer. It made her curious about the kind of person who did this line of work.

The circumstances that brought her to the shed came to mind. She was still furious with Reggie; she fantasized about pulling the trigger and watching his body fall limp to the ground.

Lord knows I should've shot him.

Duck came back with a cup of coffee for her.

"Here you go, miss. I didn't know if you wanted cream or sugar, but the essentials are sitting over on the countertop right there."

Ronnie took the cup from his hand and poured in two creams and one sugar. She sipped and closed her eyes in delight. "This is good."

"I told you I make a decent brew."

The pair sipped their drinks, and then he asked, "So, why were you doing target practice with the policeman?"

"You saw that?"

"Hard to miss after the first bullet. But if anyone asks, I didn't see nothing."

"Well, Duck. I appreciate your silence and the coffee." Duck chuckled and took a sip of the coffee, then asked.

"So, did he steal from you?"

"Excuse me?"

"Pastor Reggie, did he steal from you?"

"He was trying to, in a way… but I have a feeling you're talking about something else."

Duck sipped his coffee.

"You know, the reason he doesn't do funerals here anymore is because management stopped him. When people die, some of the families make sure they get buried with their favorite jewelry, gold, or diamonds, all kinds of stuff. Him and my predecessor had a deal where, before he put them in the ground, he'd take all the jewelry and drive a county or two over and pawn the stuff for cash."

"That sick mother—"

"Point is, Reggie done gave many people a reason to shoot him."

If Ronnie could dig up more information on Reggie, it could help her cause. She decided to press the issue. "So you know Reggie?"

"Small town, hard not to, the way the man goes around beating his chest."

"You know Reggie well then. Sanctimonious son of a bitch."

"Is that why you tried to give him a new hole in his hind parts?"

Ronnie chuckled. "He and I had a disagreement."

"Well, it's your business to keep. The less I know, the better. But, can I give you a piece of advice?"

"Sure, I'll bite."

"Men who are used to power don't like to feel powerless. The way you had him hightailing it out of here, it's not a matter of if, but when, he decides to get even. Watch yourself."

Ronnie nodded in agreement. "I'll keep that in mind. Thank you for the coffee, Duck."

After farewelling the groundskeeper, Ronnie got back in her car, deciding to retrieve Reggie's pistol and drop it off with Devon before she left town. Once she got in the car she called her friend.

"Hey, Ronnie, where are you?"

"I'm about to leave town, Dev. Before I go, I need to give you something."

"Okay, wanna come by the station?"

"I'd prefer not to."

"Okay, where do you want to meet?"

"I'll meet you at the gas station up the road from the station. I should be there in ten."

"I'll see you there."

The short drive to the gas station gave her the time to think back on her conversation with her mother, making peace with herself.

It wasn't long before she arrived and saw Devon in a charcoal suit waiting on her.

She parked the car and got out. "Looking good, Triple D. Is that your partner?"

"Hey, Ronnie. Yeah, that's him. What do you have?"

"I had a run in with Reggie. He lost his gun, so I'm—"

"How did he lose his gun?"

"Well, he dropped it. The point is, I'm leaving it with you."

"Where is it?"

"Passenger seat."

Dev walked over to get the gun. When he came back, he had Ronnie's purse.

She looked at him in confusion. "What are you doing?"

"Ronnie, listen to me. You need to quit talking. About twenty minutes ago, Officer Clayton was shot. Before it happened, he called dispatch and implicated you."

"That prick showed up to my mother's gravesite to—"

"Ronnie, stop talking. I'm not playing. You need to come with me and answer a few questions."

21
FACING THE CONSEQUENCES

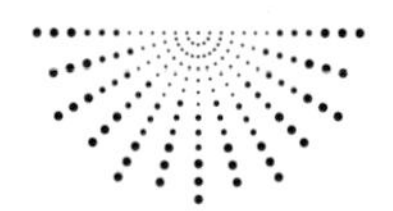

"Look, Ronnie, I want to be clear: you're not charged with anything, but your defensiveness isn't helping our investigation. It's important to cooperate, considering you threatened to kill the man in a public place just a few days ago, and now he's in hospital fighting for his life."

Ronnie took a deep breath.

While she had shot in his direction just a few hours ago, she was confident she didn't hit him. But the longer this interview went on, the more she began to doubt herself.

Did I hit him? This cannot be fucking happening.

"Just tell us where you were."

Ronnie looked at the other detective and smiled. "Lawyer."

Devon stood up and patted his partner on the back. "Give us a second, Frank."

The cop stood up and walked out of the room.

Devon sat in front of Ronnie. "Ronnie, I—"

"Go to hell, Dev. This is some foul shit."

"Ronnie, you're in some serious trouble. They think you shot a cop. Just take a gunshot residue test, and if you pass, you're free to go."

"I'm not doing a damn thing until my lawyer gets here."

"Reggie is in surgery and should come out soon. When he wakes up, if he identifies you as the shooter, it's over for you."

Ronnie sat in silence, studying her fingernails as her friend spoke. "Despite what you may think, I am trying to help you. You have my word on that."

"I didn't get this far in life believing the words of men. So, if you could do us both a favor and save your breath, because I won't say anything unless it's to my lawyer."

As Devon was about to talk, the door opened.

Ronnie's lawyer had arrived.

"Detective, my name is Alex Hughes. I need the room to have a word with my client."

Devon looked at Ronnie then back at Alex. "She's all yours."

Alex took a seat and Ronnie gave her a rundown of everything that had occurred. A moment later, Alex inquired. "You're positive you didn't shoot him?"

"Ninety percent sure."

"Close enough. Let's get you out of here."

Alex rose and signaled for the officers to come back. Opposite Ronnie and Alex, the group took their seats at the steel table.

"Well, my client is waiting," Alex said.

"Waiting on what?"

"On your questions. She's not under arrest. We'll voluntarily answer your questions."

Devon shared a look with his partner, both of them shifting uncomfortably.

He placed his mug of coffee on the table. "Okay, why don't you want to take a GSR test?"

"Don't answer that," Alex interjected. Devon took a sigh and looked at his partner who then asked.

"Where were you earlier?"

"She was at her mother's grave, grieving."

The cops shared another look before Frank asked, "Okay. What took so long for you to grieve?"

"Stupid question, and irrelevant," Alex interjected again. "Now,

Officer, are you going to ask any questions relevant to your investigation, or is my client free to leave?"

"She can't leave." Devon insisted. Alex waved her hand dismissively.

"In the time we've been sitting here, you've shown not one scrap of evidence, nor offered a motive."

Damn, she's good. Ronnie thought.

Frank tapped the folder sitting on the table in front of him. "I don't think you understand. Your client is in a lot of trouble. The motive is that your client was angry because Officer Clayton was selling her mother's house."

Alex looked at Ronnie and then at detectives in disbelief and chuckled. "Is that it? For shits and giggles, how much is the house worth?"

"Two hundred thousand."

Both women rolled their eyes. "You've got to be kidding me." Alex scoffed. "Listen, Dumb and Dumber, my retainer is more than twice that. My client could buy this town three times over. She is not hurting for money."

"Your client also slapped the victim at a funeral." Devon interjected.

"She got the holy spirit and laid hands on him."

"She threatened his life at an outpatient rehabilitation center right before he was shot."

Alex appeared bored as she studied her cuticles. "Your point?" she pressed. Frank then said.

"She was seen buying a gun, the same caliber used on the victim. The vendor who sold the gun said she not only tipped him, but said, and I quote, 'I'm looking for something to blow a motherfucker's head off'. All of this in the last forty-eight hours."

"Again, I'm not seeing your point." Alex fired back.

Devon rubbed his head in frustration. "We found her with not only her own weapon, but Officer Clayton's gun in her purse."

Alex looked at the two of them blankly, then back at Ronnie. "Let's go Veronica, we're leaving."

The pair stood up and headed towards the door when Devon stood up and stepped in front of them. "Just wait a moment now. We still have questions."

"No, what you have is circumstantial evidence that has nothing to do with my client. If you want to find out who shot Officer Clayton, either ask him yourself, or do your job. Until then, we're leaving."

"You're not going anywhere. Sit down," Devon ordered.

Alex smirked, and examined Devon. Then walked closer to him and said. "Detective Flynn, you don't know me, so you're not aware that I'll chew this entire case up and use your career as dental floss. If you don't want to gamble your livelihood on a string of circumstantial evidence, we're walking out that door. Unless you want to explain under oath why you didn't press charges after Officer Clayton arrested my client yesterday?"

"Excuse me?"

"You know, when my client got the holy spirit at the funeral and you told her to be careful. Why did you tell her that?"

"I...uh, I—"

"As an officer of the law, is it commonplace to release assault suspects already in your custody?"

Devon remained silent. Alex persisted.

"It's also funny that, within twenty-four hours of the incident, Officer Flynn was promoted to detective, and he's now working this case."

"My promotion had nothing to do with it."

"Are you sure? Beyond a reasonable doubt?" Alex asked.

Both detectives were silent.

"Here's what I do know," Alex continued. "You have no physical evidence, no eyewitnesses and a shaky motive at best. Compare that to my evidence: an alibi. The only question that remains is: are you going to throw your career away defending a cop we both know has crossed lines we're not even aware of, or are you going to get the hell out my way?"

Devon opened his mouth to respond when there was a knock on the door.

He turned around and walked outside to meet another officer, who whispered to him. Both Ronnie and her lawyer looked at each other, puzzled.

After a moment, Devon came back in. "Ronnie Duvalle, you're free to go."

Ronnie sat up. "Really?"

"You sound surprised."

"I am, only at the fact that someone here actually did their job."

Ronnie and Alex got up, and Ronnie addressed the detectives. "You held me in this room for the last few hours because you thought I was the suspect. Are you not going to at least tell me who shot the man?"

Devon looked at his partner, and then back at Ronnie. He was about to respond when two police officers walked by the open door with Chief Stevens in cuffs.

Frank answered her question, ignoring the shock on everybody's faces. "Chief Stevens confessed. Pastor Clayton allegedly assaulted his daughter, and he attacked the pastor."

"Would you listen to that? An actual motive. I'm starting to wonder if anyone in this town has any damn sense."

Alex chimed in. "Well, if that's all, I'm going to get back home and work on the Kimble case."

"Thanks, girl, I'll call you." She walked with Alex to the front door of the police station. After their farewell, Ronnie was headed to her car when Devon caught up to her.

"Hey Ronnie, wait up."

"Not now, Triple D."

Devon scurried in front of her, blocking her path. "Listen, I'm sorry about the way—"

"You know what, Devon? For a moment I thought I actually had a friend in this town. Yet the first moment you get a little taste of power, you pull this shit?"

"Ronnie, ever since you've come back to town, you've been a plain old bitch. And I let it go because I missed my friend. I've always had your back. I'm even giving you some leeway on the shit that's coming out of your mouth right now. But make no mistake about it, my job is just as important to me as yours is."

"Oh, you made that—"

"I'm not done. I convinced them not to come at you with guns blazing. I told you immediately to stop talking. Hell, I tried to help as much as I could in there, and I'm not gonna tolerate disrespect from you."

"You played me, Dev! You knew what I was up against, and you didn't warn me. What kind of friend is that?"

"Ronnie, you had his gun, and I had a job to do. All you had to do was tell me the truth."

"I told you the truth when I told you I didn't shoot him. But was that good enough? No, you had to show off in front of your partner like you were auditioning for Law and Order Breaux Bridge."

"I'm not him."

"Excuse me?"

"I'm not the guy who shot your fiancé. I'm Devon Flynn. I did my job properly."

"My fiancé's situation has nothing to do with this."

"Are you sure? Because we followed the clues—"

"You hid behind your blue wall."

"Ronnie, he called in and said he was being shot at by you."

Ronnie scoffed at him. "That should've been your first clue. The man is a liar."

"And you're not? You just sat in that interrogation room and said you 'caught the holy spirit'."

Ronnie was silent. After a spell, she said, "Well, technically Alex said that."

"It doesn't matter. Look, I know you have a big fancy life in Houston, and this little swamp doesn't mean anything to you, but this is my home. It's where I met Rue and you. I'm damn proud of what I do, and I'm not gonna let you or anyone else tell me how to do it."

"It's just a place, Devon! There are a million other shitty little towns just like this one, and nobody's forcing you to live and die in the same five-mile radius," she fired back. She stepped closer to her friend and looked him in the eyes. "You know what your problem is? You don't take life by the horns; you wait for life to happen to you."

"What in the hell is that supposed to mean?"

"It means that you want to sit around and pine away, waiting for a woman you don't have the balls to approach. You think I ran from Breaux Bridge, and you're right – there was nothing here for me. It had nothing to do with my shitty childhood, or my issues with my family. I was meant for more than this town, and you are, too. You're just too afraid to go after it. You want Rue? Then tell her how you feel. You want to be a detective? Fine, go to a real city and be a goddamn detective, not some glorified security guard, because believe me, as long as you stay in this one-road town, that's all you'll ever be."

The two sat silently in their tension.

After a moment, Devon said, "Listen, I have to go in and take Chief Stevens' statement. Are we cool?"

Ronnie heaved a giant sigh. "Tell me what you know about Rue giving him the money and we're good."

"I just found out about it when we were running everyone's finances—"

"To build a case against me."

"Well, yeah. Apparently she's taking some of the life insurance money she got to help Reggie out of whatever he's gotten himself into."

"She can't be this stupid."

"Yeah, well, that's all I know. Are we cool?"

Ronnie rolled her eyes then exchanged a fist bump with her oldest friend. "We're good. Now let me go stop this idiot sister of mine."

She left her friend and walked to her car.

I have to stop Rue before it's too late.

well now she gonna need life insurance money to pay his Dr bills

22
BEHIND CLOSED DOORS

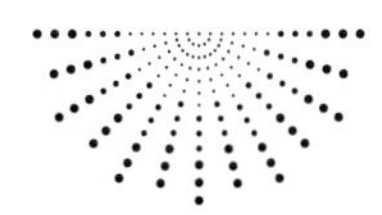

Lord knows, I hate hospitals.

It wasn't long ago she was rushing to a hospital to deal with her own gunshot victim.

Can't think about that now.

She needed to ignore her emotions; her sister was far too gullible, and would cave to Reggie's request for the money. She couldn't let that happen.

She raced to Reggie's room. When she got there, she found her sister with Pastor Reggie, who was awake and lucid. Rue was sitting in the seat by his bed, holding the paperwork.

Ronnie sneered at him. "I see you found a way around selling my momma's house."

"Ronnie, you better be glad I took one in the leg, because soon as I get out of here, I'm putting my foot up your ass."

"I'd love to see you try, you son of a—"

"Stop it right now!" Rue yelled. "Like it or not, we're a family. When one of us needs help, we gotta be there for each other."

Rue pulled out a pen. Ronnie looked at her sister blankly.

"Rue, just what in the hell are you doing?"

"Ronnie, stay out of this," Reggie chimed in.

"He's using you. It's all he knows how to do."

"I'm going to help him, Ronnie. I have the money." Rue replied.

Ronnie walked over to her sister and sat in the chair next to her. "Rue, listen, I know this man has a hold on you, but believe me when I tell you, this is the biggest mistake you'll ever make."

"Stay out of this, Ronnie. This is between me and Rue."

Ronnie turned to him. "Go to hell, Reggie, you piece of shit."

She faced Rue again. "Rue, just listen to me. You're stronger than this; stronger than the hell he put us through. Do not bail this man out of anything. I've done some digging. He's bled his pension dry, and he tried to sell Momma's house. That's why he's coming to you. This isn't the Lord's will, this is Reggie's manipulation. You have to see that. He's taken so much already. Don't let him take this."

Rue studied her sister, before looking at Reggie.

Reggie smiled, beckoning for the check, as Ronnie shook her head in disbelief. She didn't want this to be her problem, but she loved her sister. She couldn't let this stand.

Rue was about to hand him the check when she hesitated. "You know, it just occurred to me that, with the police chief going to jail for shooting you, you're in a prime position to move his daughter's investigation in any way you see fit. So, I have to know, did you touch Sarah Ann?"

"Say what?"

"I asked, did you try to touch Sarah Ann?"

"Rue, I don't have time for your nonsense. I need to get that check over to the bank by close of business today. Give me the damn check."

"I'm not giving you a dime until you answer my question. Did you touch her?"

"I didn't touch Sarah Ann! Hell, I was halfway 'cross town fussing with that little creature over there when all that happened. This is all a big misunderstanding."

"So you didn't touch her?"

"No!"

"Did you touch me?"

Rue's statement was met with a sharp silence. She smiled slightly, a tear rolling down her cheek.

Reggie stammered. "Rue…I, I—"

"This is a fine opportunity to witness the Lord's judgment first-hand. Let me paint you a picture, Reggie Clayton. You're in here because you have no friends left on the high-and-mighty police force – in this whole town, in fact. As far as Breaux Bridge is concerned, you're a dead man. Because even if you didn't do it, no one will ever believe you now."

Ronnie looked at her sister in confusion as Rue wiped a tear from her eye and continued.

"I remember the first time I went to Chief Stevens and told him what you did to me. He patted me on the head and said he'd look into it. I believed him. Until you came home from your shift and forced yourself on top of me again. When you were done, and I was a shivering pile of broken bones and a bloody mess, you said something precious – something I'll never forget. Do you remember what you said, Daddy?"

Rue paced the room, like a vulture hovering over a piece of decayed meat, Reggie's narrowed eyes following her every move.

"Oh, come now, Reggie, man up! Tell the Lord what you said."

"Rue, you're no—"

"You said, and I repeat, 'No one's ever gonna believe you, because the blacker you are, the less the police care.'"

She delighted at the recognition in his eyes as he recalled that day.

"It took years to fully understand what you meant that night, but I never forgot that lesson. So let's look at the facts: earlier today, a black man around six-foot-two tried to assault a pretty, white seventeen-year-old girl. He didn't do much, but he scared her just enough to make her feel like she was in danger. The girl couldn't identify the man, but she knew one thing: he wore a unique cologne, which she'd later identify as Nautica – your signature scent, and the kind I paid my butler's older uncle $50k to wear when he grabbed little Sarah Ann."

"You…you set me up?" Reggie asked, confused by what he was hearing.

Rue smirked. "Oh, we're just getting started, Reggie. See, you were right; no one actually cares if you assault a dark-skinned girl in this town, but touch one hair on a pretty little white girl? Well, look at where we are now."

"You motherfucker! You set me up. Ronnie, call Devon and—"

"Why the hell would she help you? She tried to shoot you! Wake up, you fool." Ronnie, now aware of the gravity of the situation, turned to her sister and said.

"Hey, Rue. Maybe we should—"

"Not now, Ronnie," she barked. She glared at Reggie and continued. "You think anyone is gonna help you right now, Reggie Clayton? You're as stupid as you are dumb."

He looked for the nurse's button frantically.

Rue smiled. "You won't find it. I hid it before you woke up."

"Help! Somebody help me!"

Rue sat on the bed next to Reggie's leg and reached in her purse. As she rummaged inside, she mused, and said, "You know, I spent a lot of time in this hospital when Malcolm got sick. One thing I learned was, these walls are pretty damn thick. One time I forgot my phone in the car, and when I came back in I started talking to one of the nurses. Well, come to find out Malcolm had fallen out of his bed and been screaming at the top of his lungs for about fifteen minutes."

Reggie ignored her and continued to call for help. Rue continued.

"The other thing I learned was, they only check on their patient's every hour or so. Hell, even if you did have that nurse's button, it'd probably still take around thirty minutes."

Rue finally pulled a long needle from her purse.

Ronnie's eyes widened. "Rue, what are you doing?"

Her question was ignored. "You know, I really loved Malcolm. He was one of the best men I've ever met. I stayed by his side when he got sick, but I got tired of wiping his ass, and feeding him protein shakes, and making sure his oxygen levels were good. One day last week I thought, *what if I just didn't do any of it?*"

Bitch what!?
Murderer!

"Rue!" Ronnie gasped.

"So, you know what I did, Reggie? I turned off his oxygen. There was a moment when he looked at me, and I hesitated. But I knew if I didn't do it, I'd be wiping his ass for years to come. No one should have to wipe a grown man's ass." Reggie looked at Ronnie and pleaded.

"Ronnie, listen to me. Your sister just confessed to murder. She's going to jail, and so are you if you don't—"

Before he could finish, Rue pressed her hand on his wound, pulling an agonized scream from him.

"Now that was a scream." She giggled. "You see, Reggie? No one's running down the halls."

"Ronnie, please! You gotta help me," Reggie begged.

Ronnie turned to Rue. "Did you…kill Malcolm?"

"I did. Though I see it more as hurrying nature along. I loved that man with all my heart and I watched him die. Which brings me to my next question: if I could do that to a man I loved, just what in the hell do you think I'll do to you, Pastor?"

The room fell silent.

Rue pulled out a needle and a bottle.

"W…what are you doing?"

"I'm preparing your insulin."

"I already had my—"

Rue pressed down on his wound again, pulling another scream from him.

Stunned, all Ronnie could do was sit and watch. Rue smiled as she wiped another tear from her cheek and said.

"Reggie, there's nothing that can save you from what's about to happen. An eye for an eye, remember?"

"Rue, please," he begged.

"You took everything from me and then kicked me out on the streets like a mangy dog. So, I took everything from you; your job, your church, and your reputation. When you meet your maker, dead-broke and disgraced, I want you to remember: I'm the one who sent you back to hell."

Rue injected the insulin into his IV stream. The effects were almost immediate; he began to convulse violently.

Ronnie couldn't take her eyes off Rue, who smiled as she watched the life drain from Reggie's body.

As his eyes rolled, and his mouth foamed, Rue began to tear up as she smiled.

Still sitting in silence, Ronnie began to tear up as well. The bed stopped shaking. There was a stillness in the room that hadn't been there before.

Reggie Clayton was no more.

Y'all are some evil bitches!
Ready for the big time Rue? Help Ronnie
get revenge on the company?

23
STARTING OVER

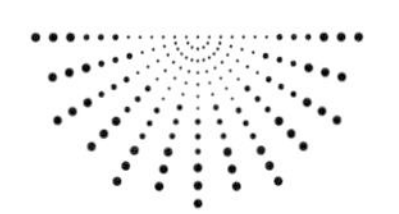

“Well, that felt better than I even imagined it would.”

Ronnie watched as Rue took an elated sigh of relief. Her sister – the passive, pleasing, doormat of a person – was not who she appeared to be.

Ronnie rose to her feet, watching in shock as her sister wiped a tear from her eye.

“Goodbye, you piece of shit.” Rue said emphatically.

Ronnie couldn’t believe her eyes. “Rue…you killed him.”

“Finally.”

“That’s not what I meant, and you know it. You planned this all along.”

“He was never getting Momma’s house or my money. He’s taken enough from us.”

Realization dawned on Ronnie. “That’s why you insisted I come to the funeral.”

“That’s not true. I wanted you to pay your respects to Malcolm. But I knew you wouldn’t be able to resist stirring up trouble with Reggie.”

“You needed him to try to follow or harass me so you could get Sarah Ann alone. You scared that girl.”

"And how do you think I felt, when that son of a bitch forced himself on me, Ronnie? Look, I don't have time for this. I'm on a very strict timeline."

Rue tucked the syringe away and hurried to the hallway, shouting for help. There were no nurses nearby. She ran to the front desk, sobbing, and a nurse dashed back with her.

After inspecting the body, the nurse turned to Rue. "I'm going to call the doctor, but I'm sorry, there's nothing we can do."

Rue crumpled to the ground in tears. The nurse knelt to comfort her when Devon walked in. Taking in the dead body in the hospital bed, he rushed to Rue and embraced her as her tears fell. "Shhh. It's okay, baby."

Ronnie was taken aback by the words and blurted out, "'Baby'? Hold up, are you two fucking?"

As the nurse led Rue to another room, Devon pulled Ronnie aside. "Look, we get it. You hated Reggie, but your sister didn't. For just one moment, can you think about someone besides yourself? The man is dead. Have some decency."

Her jaw dropped in disbelief. Not only was her sister devious, manipulative, and calculating, she was also lethal.

"Un-fucking-believable," she muttered as Devon went to console her sister. Ronnie contemplated all the measures Rue had taken to arrange everything, and was astonished. She needed more answers.

Entering the small room they'd taken over, Ronnie asked for a moment alone with Rue. Devon looked at the pair of them and stood up.

"Yeah, I gotta get back to the station and let the guys know what's going on. Stay with her, and try to have compassion," Devon said to his best friend.

Ronnie nodded in agreement.

As soon as they were alone, Rue dropped the mourning act. She wiped the moisture from her face and stood up straight, facing Ronnie, who probed, "So, are you screwing him because you like him, or are you just using him?"

"Both. I like him, and keeping him distracted was useful. I killed two birds with one—"

"You shouldn't be talking about killing two of anything right now. I can't believe you dragged me into this. Unbelievable."

Rue sighed in exasperation. "There's nothing to drag you into. You're overreacting."

"You don't know Devon like I do."

"You're right. I know him better."

Ronnie shook her head dismissively. "Why the chief?"

"Because he knew what happened to me, and knowing and doing nothing makes you just as culpable as doing the crime yourself – something you should think about."

"Me? I didn't know what Reggie did to you."

"That's not what I'm talking about. I'm talking about what happened in there." She motioned in the direction of Reggie's hospital room.

"But I didn't do anything."

"Exactly my point."

"Excuse me? I didn't just kill a man in cold blood—"

"Nor did you stop me. You wanted that son of a bitch dead just as badly as I did."

"I—"

"You saw me pick up the syringe and inject him and you saw me smile as the life withdrew from his eyes. Why do you think that is, Veronica? Like it or not, you're just like me. Most people are. Do you think anyone is going to miss Reggie? The answer is no. It's a good thing his miserable existence is over. You can pretend to be as outraged as you want, but I know you don't feel one ounce of guilt, because I don't either."

"I'm nothing like you, Rue."

"Oh, that's right, you've got a bun in your oven, so you're better than me. Is that what you tell yourself, *chère*?"

"I may be a lot of things, but I am not a killer."

"But you wanted him dead, didn't you? You've always wanted him dead. And more to the point, you didn't stop me from doing it. But your time will come, won't it?"

Ronnie shuffled in her chair to alleviate her uneasiness.

"Silence fills the air!" Rue said mockingly.

"What are you babbling on about now, Rue?"

"Do you think I'm stupid, or are you just that high and mighty now?"

"I don't know what you're talking about," Ronnie replied.

Rue nodded and smiled. "I'm sure you don't. Or at least that's what you want me to believe. Go on – lie to me, lie to yourself. It's all the same. Eventually, the truth will come out."

Ronnie waved her hand dismissively. "You're not thinking clearly."

"I know why you went to Houston, Ronnie. I know your little secret."

Ronnie's eyes widened, overwhelmed by her anxiousness. "Rue, I—"

"Oh, save it for someone who gives a damn. I'm not going to say a word, because I want to see if you have it in you."

Her sister paced the room like a panther on the prowl.

Ronnie tried to conceal her emotions, but Rue was more aware of her than anyone else.

"See, you think you have the moral high-ground over me, but time will prove you're no different from me. But I am curious to watch this play out, which is why I've decided to move to Houston."

"You're what now?"

"Oh yes, honey. I need answers to my questions: what kind of mother will you be? Will you actually go through with the marriage? What are you going to do when all the little strings you've been pulling finally come together? When you finally get the chance to do what you went there to do, will you have the guts to do it?"

A NEW BEGINNING

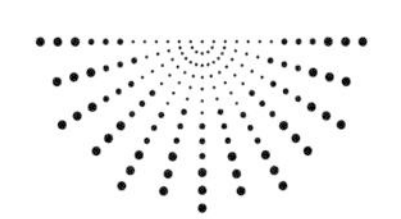

"Officer, pastor, and friend, Reggie Clayton spent his life in service. He was a leader in the community, a provider to his family, a loving husband, an officer of the law, and the heartbeat of this church. While his family feels his loss, I want them to rejoice that he is in a better place. It wouldn't surprise me one bit if God Himself met him at the gates of heaven to welcome him home," Reverend Jefferson said as he closed his sermon.

Rue smirked at the reverend's words. She wondered why they turned a blind eye to the truth.

In the end, they only had good things to say about you. She thought to herself.

The sky was gray as the reverend concluded his sermon. It would be the last sermon given at this church before its closure, due to bank repossession.

Rue was seated beside her sister and Aunt Vanessa as they listened to the last words spoken about Reggie Clayton. Neither sister had any respect for the man, but both were there to show their support for Van.

In truth, the guilt of killing him was insignificant when compared to the freedom of him being gone. Rue felt liberated for the first time. Neither physical nor mental forces confined her.

The freedom brought a smile to her face. She was taking advantage of the wind of change that was blowing in her favor. She felt like shouting out in joy, but that wasn't appropriate at a funeral; everyone in the church saw her as a devout believer.

She shouted, "Hallelujah!"

"You okay child?" Van asked.

"I'm just filled with the holy spirit, momma."

"You're full of something, alright," Ronnie muttered from her other side, but Rue didn't spare a glance at her sister. This was her chance at a new start, and she wasn't about to let it slip away. The end of the old and the beginning of the unknown.

After the service, the mourners drove their cars to the burial site to say their final goodbyes to Reggie; the same one their biological mother was buried in.

As they walked towards the grave site, Rue noticed Ronnie stopping by a tree to touch what seemed to be a fresh scratch in the tree.

"What's that about?" she questioned her sister when Ronnie caught up with them.

"Just an inside joke," she replied.

Upon arriving at the burial ground, Rue was amazed to find the police force present to give a twenty-one-gun salute. With half of the force split in their loyalty between Reggie and their chief, she wasn't sure there would be much of a turnout, but then she remembered the 'blue wall'; through thick and thin, right or wrong, Officer Clayton was one of their own.

"They sure did right by him," Vanessa said as Rue helped her to her seat.

In all her jubilation, she didn't stop to consider the woman who raised her was hurting.

As they laid the body in the ground and everyone headed their separate ways, Ronnie came over and held her aunt's hand. "Hey Momma, I just want you to know, I came because I know he meant something to you and, like it or not, you mean something to me. I'm sorry that you're sad."

Van nodded. "Well, this is as awkward a goodbye as we're gonna get. Come for one funeral, stay for two. I always loved you, Ronnie. I know you don't believe me, but I did—I do."

After a lengthy embrace, Ronnie looked to Rue. "Rue, I—"

"Did Devon tell you?"

"Tell me what?"

"He has his sights set on a position in Texas, ideally in either Dallas or Houston. Whatever you said had an effect on him."

"That's…good news, I hope. Well, I have to go. Take care of yourselves."

As the pair watched her drive off, Rue stood next to Vanessa, whose face soured as soon as Ronnie was out of view.

"Momma, what's wrong?" Vanessa turned to Rue and looked her squarely in the eyes.

"Were you in the room when Reggie died?"

"Yes, Momma, I was."

"I see."

Rue was silent, uncertain where Vanessa was taking the conversation.

Van spoke after a moment. "Valerie, something isn't right here, and I can't put my finger on it, but I'm sure that man didn't pass away naturally."

"Momma, what are you saying?"

"You care deeply for your sister, and you feel the same way about her that I felt about mine, but you can't ignore that she's done something wrong, Rue. That girl is just as venomous as her mother, and she can't see it."

Van continued while Rue stayed silent. "Reggie Clayton was a lot of things, but he was still my husband, and I loved him the same way you loved your husband. He wasn't perfect, but he was my man. He married me for richer, for poorer, in sickness, and in health, till death do us part."

"Momma, come on, let's get you back home."

"I ain't going anywhere."

Rue was shocked by the statement. She started to stumble over her words. "I—I'm not following."

"Of course you're not, baby. I don't mean nothing by this, but your brain ain't trained like that little girl that just left – like a viper. The more I think about it, the more I'm certain she had something to do with Reggie's death."

She was overwhelmed with relief that Van didn't suspect her, but anxiety quickly took over. "Come on, Momma, that's nonsense. Are you on drugs right now?"

"I haven't gone near a needle or alcohol since the nurse informed me of my husband's passing. I'm seeing things pretty clear right now."

"Momma, what are you saying?"

Vanessa glared in the direction Ronnie had left. "Everywhere that girl goes, death follows. She caused your mother's death, she probably tried to kill her fiancé, and there is no doubt in my mind that she killed Reggie Clayton."

"Momma, Ronnie is a lot of things, but a killer?"

"I know she did it. I feel it in my bones. I know that's your sister, but she took my husband away from me, and I ain't gonna rest until I make her pay for it."

No more questions, just answers

*The saga continues in **Seduction II** followed by **Money, Power & Sex II: The Scent of Deceit** coming soon!*

ABOUT THE AUTHOR

Norian Love is a best-selling author, screen-writer, songwriter, and poet, whose character rich storytelling and creative world building is swiftly setting him apart as one of the top writers in the black romance genre. His latest release, Autumn: A Love Story, was the recipient of the Association of Black Romance Writers 2021 Book of the Year Award. Autumn's complementary poetic journal, Blue: Love Letters to Fatima, also became a number one best-seller, giving him the unique distinction of having number one releases across multiple genres. He was a finalist for the 2021 Black Authors Rock, Author of the Year Award, as well as a finalist for the 2022 Romance Slam Jam Best Erotic Romance EMMA Award. He is working on completing the highly-anticipated Money, Power, & Sex series and is currently serving as the head screenwriter for the University of Houston HIV Awareness campaign.

Penning the hashtag, #blacklovematters, Norian has been garnering accolades for his work from his reviewers, fans, peers, book clubs, and several podcasts. His books are sold worldwide and are published in print, eBook, and audio formats.

To learn more, visit www.norianlove.com or follow him across most social media outlets at @norianlove.

ALSO BY NORIAN LOVE

Money, Power & Sex: A Love Story

Seduction: A Money, Power & Sex Story

Donovan: A Money Power & Sex Novella

Autumn: A Love Story

Marcus: A Money, Power & Sex Novella

Gibson: A Money, Power & Sex Short Story

Code Name: Soucouyant

Poetry

Theater of Pain

Games of the Heart

The Dawn or the Dusk

Blue: Love Letters to Fatima

Music

Autumn: A Love Story: The Soundtrack

Coming Soon

In the Case of Alexandria Hughes

Seduction II

Money, Power & Sex II: The Scent of Deceit

Made in United States
North Haven, CT
20 April 2023